Diamondlot: The Diamond Squad

Eric Hua

Published by Eric Hua, 2023.

This is a work of fiction. Similarities to real people, places, or events are entirely coincidental.

DIAMONDLOT: THE DIAMOND SQUAD

First edition. December 21, 2023.

Copyright © 2023 Eric Hua.

ISBN: 979-8223763499

Written by Eric Hua.

Table of Contents

Prologue 1
Ship Ride 5
The Visitors 7
The Dining Hall 11
Return of the King 17
Gladiator Games 19
Shadow Beast 25
Trump Card 33
Gathering 37
The Animal Caretaker and the Shopkeeper 43
The Seer 49
Town of Anjen 57
The Bodyguard 61
The Mad Scientist 67
The Bounty Hunter 73
Swarm Lord 79
Antidote 87
Legion Approaching 91
Curse 97
Turtle Isle 101
Den of the Witch 105
Truth 111
Warlock 117
Awaken 121
The Great Island Turtle 127
Brawl in Fifthguard 133
Coup 139
Double Trouble 143
Abducted 149
The Fallen 155
The Trade 161
True Power 165
Past Kings And Queens 171

Omen In the Sky	177
The Artillery	185
Attack On Fifthguard	191
Battle for the Sky	197
Battle Against the Paladin	201
King's Arrival	207
The Four United	213
Lost Soul	219
Desolator	225
King's Fall	231
Orb of Chaos	237
Sacrifice	243

This book was written for my grade 6 class of 2022/2023.

Also thank you to Nathan who designed the title page for this book!

To Savreen,

Who is capable of doing anything she puts her mind and effort to. I hope you become someone who never gives up on her goals and dreams.

— Ekbera

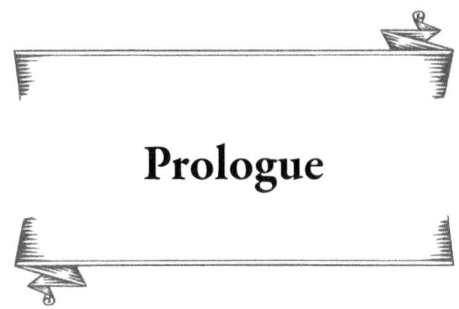

Prologue

Long ago in the realm of Diamondlot, there was a ruler known as the Mad King. Unlike how most typical kings were dressed, his outfit seemed closer to a jester than a royal monarch. But he was no laughing matter and there was very little order to his rule. What he wanted more than anything was chaos.

With his massive army of darkness, he was able to overwhelm many towns, villages, cities, and even kingdoms. Pillaging the land would not be enough to satisfy his hunger. In addition, he would claim a human from every area he conquered and turn them into one of his loyal minions. No one could stop his reign of terror.

So the forces throughout Diamondlot united together in hopes of defeating the Mad King. Led by the legendary warrior, the people of Diamondlot were able to fight back against his minions. However, the Mad King himself proved to be too much. In combination with his sword known as 'Desolator,' he completely overwhelmed most of the allied forces within Diamondlot.

Seeing only one possible course of action, the legendary hero channelled all his energy into one attack. His attempt drastically weakened the Mad King by shattering Desolator. Because of this, the king lost a tremendous amount of his power and was forced into hiding. The people of Diamondlot finally had peace in their world but it came at a heavy cost as many sacrifices were made.

A couple of centuries had passed with peace in their time, but now the Mad King's power was beginning to rise again. With the return of his army, he sent them out to reclaim his sword so he could regain his full strength. One of the greatest threats has returned and whatever the people of Diamondlot have planned, they would have to do it without the help of the legendary warrior.

2

Ship Ride

The sound of thunder crashing echoed through the boat, startling many people on it. There was a ship out at sea that was about to be caught in the middle of what sounded like a massive thunderstorm. If the storm were to manifest now, this boat would not be able to handle such an event. After all, this vessel wasn't made to carry people of high royalty, but rather transport prisoners.

The thunder woke up Bella from her slumber. She looked around to find other prisoners were awake as well. Seeing as she couldn't go back to sleep, she was about to roll off the bottom bunk of the bed when someone got her attention.

"The storm woke you up too I guess?"

"Uh, yeah." Bella still had not fully woken up. She also wasn't in the mood for conversations so she got out of her bed and made her way towards the door.

"Wait, what do you think you are doing?"

"You heard the thunder too. Aren't you at least curious as to what is happening outside?"

"You can't just leave this room whenever you want!"

"And why not?"

"Oh, you must be new here. Let me explain to you!"

The girl introduced herself as Chelsea. She explained to Bella how they were all prisoners and they were currently being transported into the gladiator arena. Select prisoners would be chosen to participate in a battle royale and fight to entertain the people. However, as of now, they were to follow orders and stay in this room. Failure to obey orders could lead to severe consequences.

Bella was impressed but also concerned that Chelsea knew so much about what was going on. Chelsea explained that she had been transported many times before. The gladiator events only happened so often, so when they weren't happening, the prisoners would be shipped back to their original locations to do other laborious jobs.

"Hey Chelsea, I hope you don't mind me asking but how did you end up here? You seem way too kind for this stinker of a place."

Chelsea explained much of her town was thrown into shambles after the invasions of the Mad King years ago. Since then, the people have fought hard to survive. But amidst all the chaos, it wasn't uncommon for people to be captured and then forced to serve others of higher standing.

While she was busy sharing her story, Chelsea looked back to where Bella was but discovered that she had disappeared. She quickly looked around the entire room and she saw Bella about to open the door and exit the room. Chelsea tried to stop her but she was too far away.

As the door opened, Bella was met with an authority figure. She stood tall with a stern face, ready to lecture Bella on her poor choice. "And where do you think you are going?"

Bella wasn't sure how to reply so immediately Chelsea jumped in to bail her out. "Sorry Warden Samantha, this is all just a big misunderstanding. She just wanted to know where the bathroom was, that's all!"

The warden looked at Chelsea who seemed very nervous then walked past her to stand in front of Bella. The entire room was staring silently, waiting for the warden to make her next move. "Tell me your name." She demanded and Bella calmly answered. She inspected Bella from head to toe and then spoke again. "I will let you off with a warning this time Bella, but I hope this doesn't become a common occurrence."

Bella remained quiet so Chelsea felt the need to speak for her, "Don't worry Warden Samantha you will never hear from her again!" The warden then turns her back to them and slams the door shut as everyone returns to what they were doing.

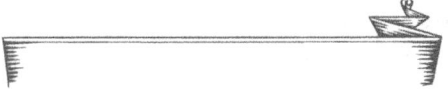

The Visitors

Away from the prisoner transport vessel, in the middle of the Kingdom of Fifthguard stood a beautiful castle. Within these walls was an elegant queen known as Queen Victoria. Though most royal figures sat back and let their advisors do everything, Victoria was different. She did her best to be involved with everything that was happening around the realm of Diamondlot in hopes of bettering the lives of all civilians.

During the past few months, Queen Victoria has had several meetings with the high council. They gathered to discuss the imminent return of the Mad King. His forces were already on the move and had struck multiple kingdoms throughout the land. Although none of the forces have been able to break through yet, many kingdoms have suffered heavy losses.

Today, Victoria was busy going over letters that were brought in from the messenger birds. She went through as many as she could with each one sounding similar and causing great concern. The letters were reports that the Mad King's forces were growing in power, while the allied forces were constantly losing their strongest warriors.

After opening about twenty of these letters, she had to pause for a moment as she felt a slight headache. As she was taking a break, there was a knock on the door and the queen allowed the person to enter. The one entering was the queen's most trusted advisor, Zoë. She walked up towards the room before bowing in respect and asking for permission to speak.

"Zoë, you know how I feel about formalities. It's just the two of us here, there is no need for you to ask permission to speak or call me Queen."

"Oh right, force of habit and it will probably happen again."

"Sigh, so what news do you have for me today?"

"Before I get to that, Victoria you need to rest. You are placing too heavy of a burden on yourself. The people need their queen but most importantly, so do the people who care about you."

Victoria took a deep breath before replying. "Thank you, Zoë for telling me that. I'm glad I have a friend like you to watch my back."

"You would do the same for me."

"So what is the news you have for me?"

"Oh right, I almost forgot. There are a couple of people who arrived at the gates this morning and requested to meet with you."

"Arrived this morning? Wait Zoë, there is a long list of people that have requested to see for months and maybe even years. If anyone else found out you broke the rules you could be severely punished."

"I'm not breaking the rules, I'm just working the system. Plus, I got you to bail me out if anything bad happens!" Victoria shook her head in disbelief and Zoë continued. "Hey, you know I wouldn't waste your time letting just anyone see you. Give me some credit!"

"You are right. I trust your judgement. So who are these two that are so important that you need to jump them ahead of everyone else?"

"They are former soldiers from the Mad King's army."

Suddenly, Victoria's mood shifted as she wasn't sure how to respond to what Zoë had said. Many questions rushed through her head: What did the two want? But most importantly, could they be trusted?

"I have already asked them to hand over all their weapons and got the guards to do a thorough search to ensure they aren't hiding anything. I will also have them escorted into this room with the elite guards."

"I shouldn't have expected anything less from you," Victoria said as she was impressed with what Zoë had done.

"Of course, I got your back. Alright, I'm sending them in!"

Entering the room with the elite guards vigilantly watching them were two warriors that formerly belonged to the Mad King's army. One was a girl, who was much taller than the boy.

"How can I help the two of you?" Asked the queen.

"We would like to discuss a very important matter with you." Replied the girl.

"Well go ahead, you have our attention," Zoë added.

"But we don't have your trust. If you keep treating us like your enemies, this will not work." The girl continued.

Victoria and Zoe looked at each other trying to figure out a solution to their dilemma. Asking the elite guards to leave the room was an extremely risky decision but if there was information the two could offer to help give them an edge against the Mad King, they had to take a chance.

However, before they could make their choice, some of the elite guards took offence to the comments made towards their queen. Out of impatience, one of them reached out and attempted to grab the girl but before he could make contact the boy instantly intercepted his arm and threw the guard against the ground.

With one of their comrades defeated, the other three soldiers stood ready to engage in battle. On the other side, the boy was more than ready to rumble but the girl restrained him until the opposition made the first move.

The situation was getting heated and Zoë wasn't sure how to keep everyone calm. Victoria on the other hand was still thinking thoroughly about her decision. After seeing how strong the boy was, she realized the two strangers could have easily barged their way into the room and demanded whatever they wanted by brute force. However, this was not the case as they agreed to put away their weapons before meeting with her.

With a simple raise of her hand, the queen commanded her soldiers to stand down and put away their weapons. The soldiers compiled and assisted their fallen comrade lying on the floor then exited the room. Once they had left, the tension that was in the room earlier had begun to dissipate.

"Forgive my guards for their rash actions. I hope you can understand with everything going on, we have to be more vigilant of late."

"A small matter. However, what I'm about to share with you will be nothing trivial. It could very well be our only chance to stop the Mad King."

"Please go on, I'm listening."

The Dining Hall

After the transport vessel made its way to the docks, the prisoners were unloaded and immediately sent to the barracks where they would be staying in preparation for the event. The first thing on all the prisoners' minds after a long journey at sea was filling their empty stomachs. They all made their way to the dining area after they were given a briefing on what their routine would look like at their new location.

The dining area was anything but high-class. After all, it was just a temporary location where gladiators gathered for the big event. If this place was well kept, the prisoners would never want to leave and that would defeat the purpose.

There was a huge line-up to receive nourishment from the cooks. Luckily Bella and Chelsea were able to beat the rush so they were able to find a table to sit together and enjoy their meal. Enjoy might have been a strong word as there wasn't much to like about the food here. They were given a tray that contained a bland-tasting soup, some overcooked mashed potatoes, and a mysterious meatloaf that seemed to have been left over since the last event.

As they sat across from each other, Chelsea spoke while Bella was gobbling down the food on her tray. "Bella, seriously the stunt you pulled back at the ship was way too risky! Who knows what punishment the warden could have put you through!" With a bunch of food stuffed in her mouth, she nods, mostly just to get Chelsea to stop scolding her.

"Sigh, well that's all done now. From now on you have to stay out of trouble. Got it?" Chelsea asked.

"Yeah yeah got it. Hey, are you going to finish that?" She asked since she was still hungry. Chelsea was stunned that Bella could put so much food into her stomach. She was about to give some of her portion over to Bella but there was a sudden commotion coming from the line-up. Immediately, they both turn their attention towards the cause of the noise.

At the front of the line, one of the prisoners was very dissatisfied with the amount of food he got on his tray. Looking next to him, he saw a girl who had a tiny bit more food on her and he demanded the chef to give him more. When the chef refused to listen, the prisoner directed his command to the girl and ordered her to hand over some of her portions.

His voice was loud and everyone watched as the boy pushed the girl aside when she refused to give her food away. Although everyone saw the atrocious act the boy had committed, no one stepped in to help the girl.

From afar Chelsea continued to watch what was happening. "I feel bad for the girl, you don't want to be messing with that guy of all people..." As Chelsea turned back to look at where Bella should be sitting, she found that she had disappeared. Immediately she looked back at where the boy was and to her dismay, she saw Bella walking up to him. "Oh no..."

The boy was about to claim all his food but before he could leave to enjoy them, his path was blocked and as he looked up, he saw Bella who stood in his way. "What are you looking at? Step aside!"

Bella stood her ground. "Give back the food you took from the girl."

"Listen, I don't know who you think you are but all I did was make sure we all got an equal fair share of the food. Her plate had a bit more so I evened it out by taking some of hers. See? Nothing but equality here."

"Tch, yeah right. If you ended up with more food on your plate you would totally go out of your way to give some to her..." Bella replied sarcastically. When she spoke back, everyone else in the room gasped.

"Alright, you are starting to get on my nerves. I'm going to..." Before he could finish his sentence, Chelsea intervened. "Oh, there's no need for that! This is just a huge misunderstanding and we don't mean any harm, Rylin." However, Chelsea's effort would be in vain as Rylin already had his intention set on striking Bella.

Right as he was about to swing his arms, the alarm in the dining hall sounded which forced everyone to stop what they were doing as the soldiers entered to take control of the scene. Bella was carefully restrained by a couple of the guards while Rylin was kept at bay by a few other guards who had their spears up.

After the situation had been contained, the warden entered the room. Warden Samantha returned and she was not pleased with what had happened. "Why am I not surprised to see you involved in this?" She looked directly at Bella.

"Warden Samantha, I apologize but it's all a big misunderstanding…" The warden held her hand up to stop Chelsea.

"Rylin I know you are excited but you of all people know the rules. No aggression outside of the arena. Have you forgotten or do you need a reminder?" Although her tone sounded kind, hidden underneath those words was a threat.

Rylin covered the scars on his left arm, hinting that he had been punished before for such an infringement. "No reminders needed," he answered reluctantly.

"Normally I wouldn't do this but you have quite an intriguing personality, Bella. This will be your final warning. Next time, you will be disciplined for your transgression." While the warden was speaking to Bella, Rylin caught wind of Bella's name and he made sure not to forget it.

"Guards, escort Rylin back to his quarters and ensure he stays there until the event tomorrow." The soldiers complied with her orders and as Rylin was about to leave the dining hall he had one thing left to say. "Heh, watch out tomorrow, I'm coming for you in the arena, Bella!"

After he was taken away, Warden Samantha also left the area and everyone dispersed to finish their food. Bella turned around to help the girl who was pushed aside by Rylin. Chelsea also rushed in to give a hand.

When Bella asked if the girl was okay, she nodded her head as she didn't seem like much of a talker. She thanked Bella for what she did and revealed that her name was Ava. "So who was that bully anyway?" Bella asked.

Ava went quiet again so Chelsea jumped in for her. "That was Rylin, and he is the reigning champion of the Gladiator Games." Chelsea's answer caught Bella by surprise. "That guy? No way! He's half my height!"

Ava nodded in agreement. "He's been the champion for three years in a row."

"Has he always been such a jerk too?" Bella asked.

"He wasn't always like that." She paused and then pulled out a drawing for Bella and Chelsea to see. The piece was tremendously drawn and it showed a picture of a boy standing up for a girl who was being made fun of for her lack of physical strength.

"What? That's the same Rylin who pushed you aside earlier? I can't believe that! What happened to him?" Bella said in shock.

"After becoming champion, the pride of winning got to him. He's been getting more overconfident with each victory and now he has been treating everyone in the games as inferiors. All that matters to him is winning and remaining the champion." Chelsea added.

"Well someone needs to knock some sense into that guy. May as well be me!" Bella stood up smacking her fists together.

"And how exactly are you going to take down the three-time champion?" Questioned Chelsea.

"Hey, don't you worry, I have a well-thought-out plan." She lied as she had no idea how she was going to beat Rylin.

"Please just don't hurt him too badly." Ava requested.

"No promises!"

Return of the King

Far away from the light that shone on the kingdom, were the dark shadowlands where even the bravest warriors fear to tread. This was where the Mad King's army lurked as they were awaiting their orders. His army consisted of various monstrosities but the bulk of the forces consisted of the small but tenacious goblins, along with the much bigger orcs.

Sitting alone on his throne, the Mad King was opening the palm of his hand. It took some time but eventually, a dark sphere began to form above his hand and he directed his focus on maintaining that power. However, as he was starting to gain control, one of the lieutenant orcs came in and disrupted his focus, and the sphere dissipated.

The Mad King immediately directed his attention at his lieutenant who was filled with fear. "My apologies supreme overlord, I didn't know you were training, please forgive me!" He begged for mercy on his knees. The Mad King got off his throne and walked until he was towered over the lieutenant. "Oh don't you worry about a thing, I can always train later!" The way he spoke was somewhat reminiscent of a jester but something about his aura gave off a dreadful presence.

"Now what was it that you wanted to tell me about?"

The orc was still sweating but he managed to explain to the Mad King that a couple of their soldiers had gone missing. They fled during the night a few days ago and they were suspected to have entered into the kingdom to possibly conspire with the enemy to stop the Mad King. When asked about their names, the lieutenant replied that the two missing soldiers were Charlotte and Nathan.

The Mad King took a bit of time to process the information before asking the orc to stand. He was still fearing for his life but he complied and rose slowly.

"Well done lieutenant! Because of your hard work, you were able to identify the two traitors within my army! You should be very proud of yourself and be promoted for such a feat!" The lieutenant was finally able to relax a bit as he slowly smiled. The Mad King then placed his hand on his shoulder. "But you should also be punished for allowing two human teenagers to escape."

A small pulse of dark energy flowed from the Mad King's arm and into the orc's body. It didn't take long before the energy spread throughout its body and within seconds, the orc was lying lifeless on the floor.

The Mad King then snapped his fingers and a group of goblins rushed into the room. The king commanded for the critters to clean up the mess and they quickly followed his orders. Once they left the room, he sat back on his throne, preparing to meditate.

"Charlotte and Nathan? I am not in the slightest bit surprised. But maybe you two could still be of use... hahahahah!"

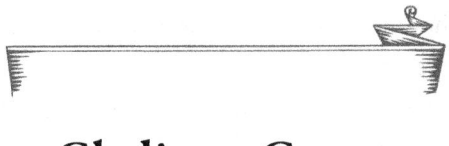

Gladiator Games

People were beginning to pour into the arena to watch the anticipated Gladiator Games. Seats were filled at an alarming rate and the soldiers were on high alert to ensure no intruders or suspicious activity would take place on such an event. Queen Victoria and her advisor Zoë were attending the event but they concealed their identities as they didn't want to draw any unnecessary attention.

"Are you sure it's a good idea to trust them with this plan? We could be putting everyone in danger if something goes wrong." Zoë wondered.

"I know, but they gave their word that if anything happened, they would intervene and protect everyone."

"Hello! We just met these two strangers! And they were originally from the forces of the Mad King!" Zoë's voice grew louder and some of the audience began to look at her, but she immediately shut her mouth and became quiet to avoid breaking her disguise.

"Indeed, they were once part of the Mad King's army, but remember they are also human. They probably want nothing more than to rid this world of the Mad King who took their lives away. I believe we can trust them." Victoria stood on her conviction.

"Blah! Fine but if something bad happens, don't say I didn't warn you." Zoë answered with a grumpy face.

On the other side of the arena, Charlotte and Nathan sat with their cloaks over their heads, waiting for the games to start.

"Hey Charlotte, why are we covering our faces? Nobody even knows who we are."

"Isn't this what all the cool kids do these days? Cover their faces and pretend not to be interested?"

"I don't know, I haven't hung around people much over the years."

"Oh right. Guess it's been a while for the both of us."

"Hey Charlotte? Do you think this is going to work? I feel this plan is too risky and makes little sense."

"The Mad King can counter any plan we throw at him if he expects it. Although this plan may seem extremely unorthodox, it's also our best chance of beating him." She explained.

"I hope you are right..."

Once the stadium was packed to its capacity, the announcer stepped into the arena at centre stage to make his introduction to the audience. "Ladies and gentlemen! Welcome all, my name is Kavan and I will be your announcer for the thirty-first Gladiator Games! Get on your feet as you are all about to witness the most exciting games in Fifthguard history! Let's take a look at our contestants this year!"

On the arena, the gates had been opened and walking into the arena from different entrances were the competitors for today's games. Bella looked around and she could see Chelsea and Ava on the other side of the battlefield. As her eyes met with Chelsea's, she remembered the conversation they had the night before.

"Alright Bella, I know you want to go after Rylin first but I advise against that."

"What? I was totally not going to do that. What made you think that was my strategy?" Chelsea just gave her an unimpressed stare. "Sigh, fine, I won't go after Rylin. Then what do you suggest, oh fearless leader?"

"You can go after Rylin, but just make sure only five contestants are remaining before you do so."

"Huh? Why five?"

"The top five finishers not only receive recognition but they also get special privileges. Think of it as an upgraded service."

"Are the rewards really that great?"

"Hey, it can't be worse than our current living conditions."

"You got a point, alright I will do as you say."

In her mind, Bella went through who she wanted to keep as the five contestants remaining. She was going to be one of them along with Chelsea of course. The third person she would want to be Ava, and the fourth would be

Rylin as she would be able to battle him with as little interference as possible. Then that just left the one remaining fighter who Bella didn't care for.

"Alright everyone, those are the thirty contestants we have for today! Rylin is the obvious favourite going for his fourth straight championship! Will he be able to accomplish that with the competition looking so fierce today? Well, that's enough for me! Contestants, ready your weapons and let the Gladiator Games BEGIN!"

(thirty minutes of battling later...)

"Ladies and gentlemen, I can hardly believe how much has happened in just thirty minutes! There are only ten contestants remaining and boy oh boy is the arena heating up! It should come as no surprise that one of the remaining gladiators is none other than the previous champion Rylin who had single-handedly taken out ten of the other contestants himself! Looks like we could potentially be in for another repeat!"

As the crowd continued to cheer, Nathan and Charlotte continued to monitor the fighting abilities of each gladiator in hopes of finding the one they were looking for.

"So Nathan, what do you think of the Gladiator Games so far? Have you noticed anything interesting?"

"I see you are testing my observation skills. I will give it a shot. If you are evaluating this battle purely from a clueless bystander standpoint, you would think Rylin would be the clear-cut winner. However, the ten contenders that he knocked out were by far the weakest of the bunch, therefore that proves nothing. Those two (Chelsea and Bella) are a bit interesting because individually they don't seem very strong but they work well together and have combined to knock out a total of five well-trained contestants."

"What about that girl who seems pretty quiet there?" Charlotte pointed to Ava.

"Honestly, I have no idea how she is still in the fight. One of the contestants had her on the ropes but somehow he tripped over something and knocked out himself. She might be the luckiest person here!"

"Better lucky than good right?"

"Pft. I don't need luck."

"So you are finished with your assessment?"

"No, there is one more person in this arena worth noting." Nathan pointed to one of the contestants who wore a hood to cover their identity. "That person over there has kept a low profile this entire fight but something is off."

"Wow, you are more perceptive than I thought. That is the same fighter I'm concerned about. Their movement is nearly undetectable and I can't get a gauge of their strength. Be on your guard, we might need to intervene."

23

Shadow Beast

The remaining ten contestants were taking their time, assessing each other before making their move. Some seemed eager to get the games over with, while others continued to be cautious. However, before the fighting could commence, Announcer Kavan had another interruption.

"Ladies and gentlemen! I know you were all anticipating a wild brawl between the final ten contestants. However, I have been given orders from Queen Victoria that when the competition has dwindled to ten contestants, there will be a special event!"

The audience looked at each other confused as did all the contestants. Bella looked to Chelsea to see if she might have any knowledge but it was clear from her body language that she didn't know either.

"Everyone hold onto your seat, as there is going to be a new contestant entering the battlefield! Give it up for the mysterious, the enigma, the one and only Jett!"

Away from the other ten contestants, a giant cage ascended from a hidden compartment on the ground. Once the cage was on ground level, a boy who wasn't too large in stature emerged from it. He also wasn't wearing any armour or carrying any weapons, leaving everyone wondering, what was so threatening about the boy.

"Uh, hi everyone? It's nice to meet you all." Jett spoke up.

Bella, Chelsea, Ava, Rylin, and the hooded contestant didn't say a word but the other five contestants were not so kind. They were furious that the Queen would waste their time by sending a weak boy into the arena. Immediately they began calling him names and pushed him aside.

While protecting himself, Jett tried to warn them, "Please, stop! I don't want it to hurt anyone!" But the five contestants wouldn't listen to him. They laughed at his warning and continued to mock and kick him. Jett endured and did his best to hold back his emotions but eventually, the pain was too much and he fainted from exhaustion.

The heartless bullies began to walk away after hurting the defenseless boy, but as they turned their backs on him, a concentrated amount of dark energy began to gather around the unconscious boy.

Suddenly, a shadow appeared out of Jett's body and it manifested into a creature of terror. It stood about ten feet tall and it looked down on the five contestants, unleashing a terrifying shriek.

The five attempted to fight back against the shadow beast by doing a split attack but they were all swatted away with ease by its arms. Seeing as their first strategy didn't work, they changed up their formation and advanced together for a combined assault.

The shadow creature did not flinch as it saw the attack coming. It was waiting for the perfect moment to unleash his counterattack. The five fighters charging at it were completely clueless and they were all about to be devoured by the creature's shadow powers, but suddenly the hooded fighter appeared in the middle of their formation.

Her appearance startled the other five fighters, which allowed her the opportunity to take them down and throw them away from the area. After the hooded fighter had successfully thrown away the contestants from danger, the shadow beast grew angry and attempted to slash the hooded fighter. The mysterious fighter managed to evade the attack, but the claw tore off her hood revealing her identity.

"Oh shoot I was hoping to keep my identity hidden for just a bit longer but no matter. Have no fear everyone, my name is Naaz, and I am the Ultimate Brawler in the entire realm of Diamondlot! This silly creature won't be any match for someone like me!" She boasted with confidence.

After hearing her boastful comment, the creature was ready for Naaz's attack. However, Rylin did not take kindly to her introduction. "Whoa whoa whoa! Excuse me, I'm the defending champion around here! You can't go around bragging like that without first challenging me to..."

With just a blink of an eye, Naaz somehow appeared right in front of Rylin and unleashed a punch that sent the defending champ flying in the air and slamming onto the ground. "Don't get up. Or I will have to use my real punch against you next time."

Bella, Chelsea and Ava were in absolute shock. Rylin the defending champion of the Gladiator Games was so easily cast aside by this unknown fighter. Naaz then walked up to the three girls but unlike Rylin, they didn't show any hostility towards her. Seeing that they were no threat to her, Naaz turned around to face the beast.

"Heh, this creature could have caused you all some major problems but luckily you got me! Don't worry, I will make short work of this..." Naaz was very confident but suddenly began to feel fatigued. Her body was feeling weak and her eyes were beginning to close. Eventually, it was too much, she slowly lay on the ground and fell into a heavy slumber.

The tables had turned. Rylin was taken out, Naaz was unconscious, and no other contestants were left to help. It was down to Bella, Chelsea, and Ava to figure out a way to defeat their enemy.

The beast was ready to strike at Naaz who was completely vulnerable. However, before it could lay a hand on her, Bella threw a pebble on its head and caught its attention. She began making faces and sticking her tongue out at it. The dark figure chased after Bella, leaving Naaz alone for Chelsea and Ava to carry and get her out of harm's way.

Bella continued running as the shadow raised its right arm and slammed it to where it anticipated Bella would be. The initial collision missed Bella but the shockwave it created knocked Bella off balance, tripping her on the ground. She tried to pull herself up but the shadows had caught up and surrounded her.

With Chelsea and Ava too far away to help, it looked like the end of the line for Bella. But Rylin rocketed back onto the battlefield and punched the hulking shadow right in the jaw. Upon his return, the audience began cheering loudly again.

"I'm the defending champion of the Gladiator Games! There is no way I would get eliminated so easily! Now I'm going to take care of this beast myself and become the champion once again!"

As Rylin recklessly charged into the fray, Chelsea and Ava made their way to Bella. Chelsea asked if Bella was injured and Bella assured her that she hadn't suffered any major wounds. However, she was extremely concerned about their current situation. She knew Rylin wouldn't be able to beat the dark beast all by himself and it seemed as though this Gladiator Games would not stop until they found a way to stop the shadow beast.

Bella turned to the both of them and spoke seriously. Knowing Ava was less inclined to fight, she asked her to stay hidden and keep Naaz safe. Ava nodded and accepted what she was told. Bella then turned to Chelsea and asked her for help in taking down their gruelling foe.

"What?! You think the two of us can beat that thing?!" Chelsea said in shock.

"Don't worry, you don't have to get close to him. I will be doing that."

"Oh. Then what do you need me for?" Chelsea wondered.

"Bait."

Rylin fought his hardest but his endurance could not keep up with the shadow beast. With another swipe of its arm, Rylin was sent slamming hard against the wall of the arena. While Rylin struggled to move, the creature raised its arm again to finish the job.

That was when Chelsea jumped in and taunted the beast. It immediately took the bait and ran after Chelsea who was regretting her decision. "Why did I agree to do this? You owe me big time Bella!" She said to herself as she ran away. With its attention focused on Chelsea, Bella was able to assist Rylin.

"Hey, what do you think you are doing?!" cried Rylin.

"Uh, what does it look like? I'm helping you." Bella replied.

"Psh! I am the defending champion of the Gladiator Games and the champion does not need any help!"

Bella had enough of his boasting. She slapped him in the face and then grabbed him by the collar. "Listen, I could care less about becoming the champion. You can have your stupid title. I just want to make sure me and my friends all get out of this alive! So are you going to help or are you going to keep being a baby?"

It seemed Bella had gotten through to Rylin. "How are we going to beat that thing?"

"We go for its vitals. Every creature has a weakness and I bet it's right where the heart is"

Bella's idea made sense but Rylin wasn't sure how they were going to accomplish the task. That was when Bella told him that she would distract the beast, allowing Rylin the opportunity to finish the job while it was distracted.

Right before they separated into their positions, Rylin mustered up the courage to thank Bella. She nodded and then turned back to engage the enemy.

Chelsea was still on the run but the shadow beast was closing in and it reached out its hand in an attempt to grab Chelsea. "Bella! You promised I wouldn't have to get near this thing! You better keep your promise right now because if I live through this you are going to..."

Before she could finish, Bella lunged forward with a spear in her hand and drove the spear through the shadow's hand and into the ground. With one of its hands trapped, the creature tried to slam Bella with its other hand but she evaded the attack and then grabbed another spear she had found and thrust it through the other hand and to the ground. The beast was now temporarily immobilized.

"You sure took your sweet time..." Chelsea said with an unimpressed tone.

"Haha yeah, sorry about that but don't worry we got this all handled now."

"We?"

"Rylin, finish this!"

Rylin appeared out of hiding, leaping into the air with his sword aimed directly at the enemy's heart. With all his might he charged at the heart of the beast but as the sword made contact against the shadow's skin, something was wrong. There was no heart within the beast.

Bella, Chelsea and Rylin were all in disbelief as the shadow beast broke through its restraint and swatted Rylin in midair. It then turned its attention to Bella, preparing to slam its fist over her head. Bella was completely frozen and couldn't move but Chelsea jumped in to push her out of harm's way. When the shadow fiend's fist made contact with the ground, the force sent Bella flying to the far side of the coliseum.

Thankfully, Bella didn't sustain any major injuries but she was now worried about what might have happened to Chelsea. She bounced back up and looked at where the impact was made and saw that Chelsea was trapped as the debris of rocks was over her body, leaving her vulnerable for the shadow fiend to finish her off.

However, when Bella looked over at the shadow monster, she saw that it was just waiting there. She was confused as to why their enemy wasn't ending the fight and that was when Bella realized what was going on. She remembered the positioning of the shadow creature throughout the battle and not once did it venture far away from Jett.

Bella grabbed one of the spears on the ground and began running straight toward her new target. The shadow creature threw both its fists at Bella but with her determination and focus, she somehow avoided both the attacks. She then slid the remaining way until she made it to Jett who was unable to defend himself.

Staring down at the human who unleashed the shadow creature, she was ready to end it all. She turned Jett around before using her weapon but the instant she saw Jett's face her focus wavered and she was unable to deliver the finishing blow. She stood there at a loss of what to do, but behind her was the shadow beast that was ready to crush her within its grip.

Bella came within inches of being crushed by the shadow's grip but a lasso looped around her body and with a sudden tug, she was pulled to safety. Bella looked up to see that Chelsea had bailed her out again.

"What happened? You had the chance to take out the boy. Why did you stop?"

"I couldn't do it. The look on his face, I can tell he was trying to control the beast from hurting people. I'm sorry Chelsea…"

"Sigh, what's done is done. Let's just find a way to stay alive."

31

Trump Card

The shadow beast continued its rampage, which was beginning to scare off some of the audience. Some made their way to the exit, fearing the situation would only get worse. But despite the fury of the shadow monster, Charlotte and Nathan continued to watch the battle.

"Looks like they are in quite the predicament. Shall I intervene and rescue them?" Asked Nathan.

"Hold on. This battle isn't over yet." Charlotte replied.

"Not over?! Those two are at their wit's end and that creature still has an insane amount of stamina left. There is no way they could pull it off!"

"Looks can be deceiving. They still have one trump card left."

"What is this nonsense you are talking about?"

"Just watch and see."

Back on the battlefield, Chelsea and Bella had narrowly escaped a brutal assault from the shadow creature and all their injuries were starting to pile up. It wouldn't take much for their enemy to end the match. The shadow beast began to charge in to take out both the girls but midway it sensed something was wrong. Looking behind to where Jett was, it saw that Rylin had eluded its senses and was within striking distance of Jett.

Seeing Jett in danger it attempted to turn around and rush to his aid but Chelsea threw her lasso and it wrapped around one of the shadow beast's arms. Alone, Chelsea wasn't enough to pull the beast back but when Bella grabbed onto the rope as well, the shadow had a difficult time struggling to break loose. Combined they knew they could hold the creature down for a couple of minutes. All their hopes were now placed on the defending champion, Rylin.

With a sword in his dominant hand, he walked up to Jett who had his hands on his head, doing his best to repress all the negative emotions. Rylin felt a bit of sympathy for him, but he couldn't let the opportunity slip away. Right here, he could end the source of the shadow beast's power and once again he would be named the champion of the gladiator games.

He raised the sword and swung it down but midway he halted his attack as someone stood in front of Jett.

"Ava? Step away from the boy!" However, Ava wouldn't move. "Ava, there is no time for games. Move this instance or I will consider you my enemy." Again she stood her ground.

Leaving him no choice, Rylin swung his sword again but he stopped as Ava held out a drawing before his eyes. It was a simple drawing of a boy defending a girl who was being bullied by others. Seeing the drawing brought back memories and calmed Rylin down.

"I still don't understand. Why are you doing this Ava?"

"Because you are a good person with a kind heart. If you take the life of this innocent boy you would never be the same. You might even turn into a monster, like the very thing you are trying to destroy now."

Rylin fell to his knees as he knew Ava was right but he was also heavily conflicted. "But how are we going to defeat that creature without hurting him?"

"Don't worry! Just leave it to me!" She said with a smile.

As Ava was making her way to Jett, Rylin could hear shouting coming from behind him. It was Bella and Chelsea who were trying to warn them that they could no longer restrain the enraged shadow. The shadow broke free, knocking Chelsea and Bella off balance. It was dashing to where Ava was heading but Rylin quickly jumped in to stall for time.

Ava was now standing beside Jett who was still in a power struggle with his mind. She lowered herself and placed one of her hands on his shoulder. Instantly, Jett felt a sudden calmness through his body. "You can rest now, there's no longer any need to fight."

With those words, the negative emotions began to leave Jett's mind. Behind Ava was the hand of the enraged shadow that was inches away from crushing her but it was now frozen and slowly it began to deteriorate as Jett's mind was clearing and now he was able to rest.

Once the shadows had disappeared, everyone in the audience including Announcer Kavan was left in a state of confusion. That was when Queen

Victoria finally revealed herself to Kavan and told him to announce the end of the Gladiator Games.

"Ladies and Gentlemen! What an insane turn of events! Somehow the menacing shadow creature has been defeated! To cap off such a wild event, the Queen has declared that there will be multiple champions this year! Give it up for your four new champions!"

The spotlight was on four remaining warriors still standing in the arena: Ava, Rylin, Chelsea, and Bella. However, Bella and Chelsea were still trying to figure out what had just happened. But they wouldn't have much time to think as appearing before them was Zoë, followed by a small group of the kingdom's elite guards.

"The queen would like to have a word with you all."

Although she said it kindly, the sight of the elite guards behind her made it seem more threatening. Without much of a choice, the four made their way to meet with the queen.

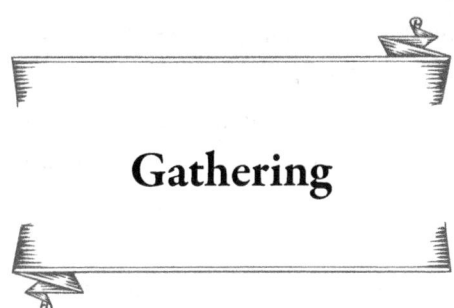

Gathering

The four were gathered in a large fancy room that was used for council meetings. They waited for a moment before a woman in a royal outfit was escorted by Zoë. Immediately the guards in the room, Ava, Chelsea, and even Rylin kneeled in respect of the queen. The only one still standing cluelessly was Bella.

"Pst Chelsea, who's that lady with the funny-looking dress?" Bella whispered. Chelsea reacted quickly by dragging Bella down to her knees.

Once she was in her seat, she asked for everyone to rise so she could speak to them. "Brave warriors of the Gladiator Games, I must congratulate you all for saving the event this year. Jett and his enraged shadow were a tremendously difficult opponent and I had concerns when I allowed for his release, that your lives might have been in grave danger.

"Wait, you were the one who sent that crazy monster against us? What kind of crazy queen are you?!" Bella yelled out of turn. Suddenly all eyes were on her as she had completely interrupted the Queen.

Zoë was ready to scold Bella for speaking without permission but Queen Victoria held her back. "No, it's fine. She has every right to be mad..." She wanted to speak further but Charlotte and Nathan entered the room, causing her to stop.

"You can stop harbouring your hate towards the queen. I was the one who convinced her to release Jett into the Gladiator Games." Charlotte spoke with confidence.

"So you are the one blackmailing the Queen!" Rylin shouted. "Have no fear your majesty, I, Rylin, the champion of the Gladiator Games will deal with this person for you!" Rylin rushed in with intense bravery but before he could lay a hand on Charlotte, Nathan appeared in front of him and sent him flying back against the wall of the council room.

The champion was knocked unconscious but thankfully there were no injuries except to his pride. Everyone, especially Chelsea and Bella looked upon Nathan in shock, wondering how such a tiny warrior could possess such strength. After showing off a small display of his power, Charlotte told Nathan that it was enough and he listened by taking a step back.

"As I was saying, I was the one who asked the Queen to release the enraged shadow upon you during the Gladiator Games. I know it sounds horrible but an even greater terror is about to befall us. If you couldn't even handle that creature, then you wouldn't stand a chance for what's coming."

She summarized what happened in the great battle between the Mad King and the legendary warrior. In the warrior's final attempt to save the people of Diamondlot, he unleashed all the power he had to drastically weaken the Mad King but it cost him his life. However, there was still a sliver of hope because what most didn't know was that the soul of the legendary hero was still alive. The only problem was that he was separated into four pieces, each one hidden within a warrior somewhere in the realm of Diamondlot. Only by gathering the four warriors together could they stand a chance against the Mad King and his dreadful army.

Bella was still confused as to how any of this related to her current situation. Charlotte explained that she needed to assemble a special team to help search for the four warriors. The team would have to be competent enough to handle themselves but they couldn't be too highly skilled because they would draw attention to the Mad King who would eventually search them out.

The Gladiator Games was used to determine which fighters Charlotte could rely on for such a difficult task. Chelsea wasn't sure how to handle what she had been told while Bella just stood there with a serious look on her face. Bella then walked up to Charlotte and began to speak.

"So let me see if I got this right, crazy lady. First, you put us up against that terrifying creature that could have taken our lives. Now you are asking us to embark on a wild search for these special warriors with extremely low chances of success and near-certain death?"

"That is correct," Charlotte replied calmly.

"Alright, count me in!" Bella smiled as she agreed.

"Wait what?! Hold on! I did not agree to this! I don't know her!" Chelsea refused.

"Perfect! You two will join Nathan and embark on your journey as soon as you are done here."

Charlotte left Nathan with the two girls and began walking away. Everyone else looked on as they were wondering where the mysterious girl was headed.

"Hey, are you just going to leave us here?" Bella asked in disappointment.

"The queen and her advisor will tell you what your next steps are. I have an important mission to complete."

Again she was attempting to rush out of the room but Chelsea stood in front of her this time.

"What is it now? Do I need to guide you through everything? Didn't think I was dealing with children here." Charlotte was a bit annoyed.

"Don't give me that! You haven't even told us what those people we are looking for would look like! If you are going to throw me into this absurd excursion, I would like a bit more information!" Chelsea demanded in frustration.

"Sigh, fair enough. Remember the other contestant with you during the Gladiator Games?"

"You mean that overconfident and headstrong fighter? What was her name again?" Bella had some trouble remembering but Chelsea reminded her that it was Naaz.

"If you were paying attention she had a mark that was beginning to glow on her hand. That mark will be the indicator of what you are looking for."

"Wait a minute, you sent one of those warriors during the Gladiator Games?! You must really want to kill us!" Chelsea concluded.

"That was a surprise. Neither Nathan nor I could have predicted that one of the warriors would appear at the games. That's why we had to take precautions and interfere a bit."

Bella was confused but Chelsea knew what she was referring to. During the battle within the coliseum, it was Charlotte who threw a sleeping dart to knock Naaz into a deep slumber.

"Now, if you don't have any further questions I will be taking my leave." She was about to disappear but she stopped for a moment. "Oh and do your best to stay alive. It will give us a better chance of winning this war."

As Charlotte left the room, Chelsea finally expressed her thoughts. "The nerve of that woman! How could she treat us like that? If that's how she treats people she just met, I hate to see how she treats people close to her!"

"My apologies for how she treated you. I didn't know she was going to be so candid." The Queen spoke.

"Forgive me for asking Your Majesty, but you are the queen! Why are you allowing that condescending person to do as she pleases?" Questioned Chelsea.

The Queen was about to reply but Zoë interjected on her behalf. "Her majesty has been through much today. Guards, please ensure our queen returns safely to her chambers and gets the rest she needs."

"No Zoë, what are you doing? There is still much to do. I still need to…"

"You need to get some sleep. You have done nothing but work and stress about this matter for months."

"But I…"

"Save it! As your most trusted advisor, I'm advising you to go to bed!"

"Alright, I will listen. Just make sure you introduce them to Sebastian and Guranjan."

She acknowledged and confirmed what the Queen asked of her. After receiving assurance from Zoë, Victoria followed the soldiers back to her chamber. That left Zoë with the newly formed team of Chelsea, Bella, and Nathan.

"Alright you three, follow me!"

The Animal Caretaker and the Shopkeeper

Back in the throne room of the shadowlands, the Mad King was quietly sitting down to focus on his meditation. As he was still in deep focus, one of his orc minions entered the room and disrupted his meditation. The orc then bowed down in the king's presence and notified him that three of his elite soldiers were waiting to enter.

The orc was about to turn around and let the elites in but the Mad King told his lackey to wait. He slowly gets up from his meditation stance and walks to the orc who is beginning to feel nervous.

"Tell me my loyal subject. Have you ever meditated before?"

"No your highness..."

"Oh? That is quite unfortunate. It's something you need to experience! But you need to stay extremely still to get the full effect."

"I will give it a try after I let your loyal elites in."

"Oh, there is no need to wait that long! Here let me show you how it's done!"

The orc cowered as he was too paralyzed by fear to move. He stood still with his hands covering his face as the Mad King placed his right hand on top of his head. In seconds, the orc was turned into stone and there was no way to reverse the process.

"Hehe. Now you can experience it for all of eternity."

After he was done punishing the orc, his three elite soldiers entered the room. They were all relatively the same size and height but they had some defining features about them. One had bugs flying around his body. Another held a staff with a skull at the top of it. And the last one held a giant scythe.

"I have a task for all of you."

Back within the city of Fifthguard, Zoë took Bella, Chelsea and Nathan through the bazaar. There were many shops here for people to barter for different goods. But they were not there to trade with the multitude of vendors, Zoë had specific people in mind for them to see.

She brought them into a store where they were met with Guranjan, a kind and always smiling shopkeeper. She greeted the three warriors as they entered and she allowed them to browse through her store filled with goods. The store was filled with a variety of items from potions, food, crafting material, scrolls, a variety of armour, weapons, and some miscellaneous items that most people have never seen before.

Bella and Nathan were so intrigued by all the items, that they began to point to the various items throughout the store asking Guranjan what they were. They alternated asking her about the items, first starting with Bella.

"What is this thing?"

"That is a skeleton's arm."

"How about this one?"

"The horn of a giant flying horn beetle."

"Okay, what about this one?"

"Ahh, that is the extremely rare, salimandizard's tail."

"Oh oh! This one this one!"

"Ahhh, that is the mythical serpent wurm's eye."

They were both star-struck initially until they realized a very important detail. Together they both asked, "Wait, how did you get all this stuff?!"

To that she replied with a smile but she never gave a clear answer. From that moment on, Nathan and Bella knew there was more to this innocent shopkeeper than meets the eye.

Chelsea felt bad for Guranjan and asked the two to focus on the task at hand. "Alright you two, quit looking at the useless stuff. Let's get what we need and leave the nice lady alone."

"It's too hard to make a choice... Why don't we just take three of everything? One for each of us!" Nathan suggested.

"Sigh, because we don't have that amount of money." Chelsea tried to explain.

"The Queen said she would be willing to purchase whatever items you will need on your quest," Zoë informed them.

When Bella and Nathan heard those words, their eyes widened and their jaws dropped. They went around the store grabbing everything they could. Chelsea watched in embarrassment as the events unfolded before her eyes.

After they were finished picking out everything, Guranjan let them know she was happy to help them and would send Queen Victoria the amount she would owe. Now that they had all the items before them, they finally realized their predicament, they didn't have enough room to store their purchases.

"Chelsea, we need your help! We bought too much stuff and we can't carry it all!" Bella said in defeat.

"Of course, you can't! That's what I have been trying to tell you this whole time! What were you two thinking?!"

"They make it look so easy in all those RPGs..." Nathan whispered.

Admitting they made a huge mistake, they allowed Chelsea to pick the necessary items they needed. A new spear for Bella, new armour for herself, food, lots of food, and water. The load that Chelsea selected was way more manageable and when they were done, they thanked Guranjan for her generosity and allowed Zoë to lead them to the next shop.

As they were about to enter and meet the next vendor, Nathan had a thought occur in his mind. "So I have been thinking. Guranjan said that a canister of water recovers more than a potion, which was created through much research and scientific study. HOW IS THAT POSSIBLE?!"

None of them had the answer and by the time they stepped into the next shop, they were immediately hit with a surprise. A flying monkey came flying towards them, forcing them all to duck their heads to prevent them from getting hit. They then looked around the store and found that the place was a zoo, literally.

There was a vast array of animals kept hidden away from the public's eyes. In addition to the flying monkey, platypus-birds were flying around, tanks filled with creatures like pig-sharks, and even interesting animals like a slug-camel. There were even more animals to list but all their attention was redirected to a man who was riding a bullboar and trying to calm it down.

They watched as the crazy bullboar frantically tried to run into walls and throw kicks around trying to injure someone. Bella, Chelsea, and Nathan all felt their lives might be in danger but the man spoke up giving them some assurance.

"Don't worry everyone, have no fear cause I, Sebastian the animal caretaker, is hereeeeeeeee!" As he finished his sentence the bullboar shook him off its back and threw him against the wall. "I'M OKAY!"

Although Sebastian was not injured, the bullboar now had its sight set on Nathan who was wearing his red cloak. "Hey! Don't give me that kind of stare! Go away! Stay back!"

The bullboar was now in hot pursuit of Nathan who was trying to outrun the wild animal. "GUYS! HELP!"

Zoë looked at Nathan running about and then looked back at Chelsea and Bella. "Are either of you going to help him?"

Bella and Chelsea looked at each other and then back at Zoë, shrugging their shoulders. So Nathan continued running full speed in circles as the three continued to watch. Thankfully, Sebastian came to his rescue, by jumping back on the bullboar's back. He grabbed some berries from his pocket and held them by his nose.

The bullboar picked up the scent of the berries and began slowing down before coming to a stop and eating the berries that were presented to him. Once the animal was calm, it went back to where it would normally lay down and Nathan could finally catch his breath.

After he handled the situation, Sebastian turned back to face his new customers. He wasn't sure they heard him before so he decided to redo his introduction. "As I was saying. My name is Sebastian, the animal caretaker and owner of this store! Welcome to my animal emporium where we find the perfect companion for you!"

When he finished his elegant introduction, Bella turned to Zoë. "So why do we need to see this guy?"

"No team is complete without a pet companion. So we are here to find one that best suits your team." Zoë answered.

"OH OH OH! THIS ONE! THIS ONE!"

"Ahh, a fine choice! This is the majestic chicken-parrot. Not only can it mimic what you say, but it has quite the habit of never staying quiet by making chicken noises." Sebastian informed Nathan.

"No way we are not taking that loud-mouth bird. Check out this one!" Bella directed their attention to another animal.

"Oh my! Also an excellent pick! That is the gorilla-bear, an extremely strong animal that is also quite stubborn and hates to listen to its owner."

Since they were only allowed to pick one, Nathan and Bella began arguing with each other over which pet they should keep. Nathan kept vying for the chicken-parrot but Bella wanted the buff gorilla-bear. Their argument was getting on Chelsea's nerves so she grabbed them both by the ear to calm them down.

It was clear neither of them was mature enough to take care of the pet anyway so Chelsea decided for them. She saw an egg, tucked away at the back of the store and asked Sebastian about it. He let her know that the egg was a complete mystery to him. He's had the egg for many years and not once had it ever shown any sign of hatching.

Although what Sebastian said should have discouraged Chelsea from selecting the mysterious egg, something about it was pulling her towards it. Trusting her instincts, she made the decision. "Animal Caretaker Sebastian, we'll take that mysterious egg!"

As he was passing ownership of the egg over to Chelsea, he had a few words to say. "Good luck hatching the egg. If it has taken me so long and still it hasn't hatched. So I can only imagine..." Before he could finish, everyone heard a cracking sound coming from Chelsea's arms. The egg was hatching!

Emerging from the shell of the egg was a cute little dragon. Sebastian couldn't believe his luck but everyone was mesmerised by the baby dragon. Chelsea embraced the new member of their team and she already had the perfect name for her, Leeloo.

With all their items prepared, Bella, Nathan, Chelsea, and their newest member, Leeloo, were led by Zoë to the gates of the kingdom. Zoë wished the team safe travels, as they journey to find one of the remaining three warriors that possessed the legendary hero's soul. Their destination is the Town of Anjen.

The Seer

The realm of Diamondlot is vast and many regions have been taken over by the Mad King's army. After conquering a village or town, the Mad King's forces might use the area as a base before moving on to their next target. And there are times when the area gets constructed into a strategic landmark. This area in particular was turned into a prison.

Within these prison walls are usually brave warriors who stood up against the Mad King's forces instead of choosing to run away. No one knows for certain why the Mad King does this. Some say he does it so he can use his mind control to convert them to his army. Others say he does it to demoralize others who resist. And then some believe he just does it because he can.

At the far North side of the prison, was a girl kept isolated from all the other prisoners. There would always be at least two guards placed specifically to monitor her station. The two orcs were on the latter half of their shift and one of them was beginning to doze off, so his partner punched him to keep him up.

"Hey! What was that for?"

"We have to stay awake. You never know what could happen!"

"Really? When has anything ever happened in the 361 times we have done this?"

"Uhhhh, there was that one time..."

"You mean the time you got scared by a rat?"

"Hey! You promised you wouldn't bring that up!"

They stopped talking for a moment before one of them turned their attention over to voice his voice frustration.

"Blah, I don't get how we get stuck with this dumb babysitting duty. That girl with a blindfold can't even see! How dangerous could this one human be?" After his little rant, he finally noticed his partner was nervously pointing at something behind him. He slowly turned around and as he saw the warden staring down at him, he cowardly apologized.

The warden wasn't impressed with their attitude but he didn't need to say anything. The expression on his face said it all. The guards stood back into position as the warden walked past them and entered the jail cell to speak with the girl.

"How nice of you to visit me."

"Ha, did your 'visions' tell you I was coming today?"

"With a stench and a grumpy voice like yours, anyone can decipher that." Her comments aggravated the warden but he refused to let it get to him.

"You are only still alive because the Mad King sees use in that future seeing powers of yours. So don't go pushing your luck!" He threatened.

"I see you are frustrated with me, but don't worry, you won't have to deal with me much longer."

"And why is that?"

"I will be leaving this place tonight."

"HAHAHAHAHAHAAAHAHAHAHAHA! And how are you going to do that? This prison is secured with guards all over and is overseen by one of the greatest wardens in the Mad King's army, ME!"

The seer didn't say anything else but gave a smile. The warden was no longer laughing but he still refused to believe what the seer had just said. He turned around, making his way towards the exit.

"Sweet dreams, because that's the only place where you will ever escape this prison!" He leaves, slamming the door shut, while the girl sits quietly without breaking her smile.

Nightfall had arrived, and a squad of four orcs escorted a prisoner who was trapped within a cage. As the cage rolled up to the entrance of the prison, some of the orcs began to speak.

"Who are you bringing in this time?"

"You won't believe it but we have the most sought-after prisoner on the Mad King's list!"

"No... you don't mean..."

"I present to you, the rebellious, the elusive, and the now captured, Charlotte!"

Despite being stuck in a cage, her name struck fear into some of the orcs. They were eventually allowed to wheel her cage in and slowly, the group of guards transported her to her new holding cell.

As they were making their way there, one of the orcs decided to taunt her further.

"I bet you want to know where we kept your friend don't you?"

Charlotte heard clearly what he said but she didn't move a muscle or show any change in her expression. Dissatisfied with her reaction, the orc hurled insults about her comrade hoping to get her to finch.

"That's enough! Just take the prisoner to her holding cell and quit fooling around!" Yelled one of the other guards.

They finally arrived near the holding cell that was designated for Charlotte. They released her from the cage and made sure the shackles stayed on her wrist. One guard stood in front while two followed behind. When she walked past the one who stood waiting for her to pass, he tried to aggravate her one last time.

"If you want to know, she is on the other side! But not like that matters, there are way too many of us to get through and you are stuck here for good!"

Once again no reaction from Charlotte as she continued to follow the lead guard to the prison cell. When they reached the holding cell, one of the guards from the back walked up to the door ready to unlock it. Right when the guard pulled out his keys, Charlotte made her move.

Without warning, she kicked the orc in front of her, which pushed him into the orc unlocking the door. The orc behind reacted by attempting to pull his weapon out but Charlotte used her shackles and bashed the orc in the face before he had a chance to draw his weapon. She then quickly pulled the key from the orc and undid the shackles on her wrist.

During this time, the orc that had taunted her had witnessed how she took out three of his allies without breaking a sweat. Charlotte gave him a death stare and immediately the orc fled in fear, desperately seeking reinforcement. He managed to escape from Charlotte's sight so he could alert the other guards.

As he found other guards throughout the prison, he urged them to rush to the cell on the other side of the prison. The instant they left, Charlotte reappeared before the orc that had taunted her. He tried to swing his weapon at her but she easily avoided his attack, tied him up with the shackles and locked him on the ground.

"Thanks for telling me where to find my friend. I appreciate your cooperation," she said with a smile.

That was when the orc realized, "You... you planned all this."

"You got it! I allowed myself to be captured so I didn't have to go through the trouble of finding this place and breaking in. Then it was a matter of finding someone who would tell me where my friend was being held. You made my job a lot easier so I will reward you by leaving you alone. I don't think the Mad King will be very happy with you though. Oh well!"

"No! Please don't leave me like this! I'll do anything!" He begged but Charlotte left him and continued into the prison to find where she needed to go.

The message eventually reached the warden who was beginning to sweat. The words of the seer from their earlier conversation could come true. With urgency, he rallied as many guards towards the cell on the northern side. As this was happening, Charlotte made her way through the prison using the vents. She followed the schematics she stole from one of the orcs she encountered and that allowed her to sneak through the area undetected.

When she reached the end of where the vent took her, she kicked off the wall vent and dropped herself in front of the prisoner in the cell. The person she had been trying to rescue was right in front of her. She pulled out the keys she stole from one of the guards and unlocked the chains on her wrist.

"Took you long enough."

"Hey! You try breaking into a heavily guarded prison by yourself!"

They could have argued longer but they could hear the orcs rushing towards their position.

"How many of them are there?" Charlotte asked.

Seert sat down in her meditation form and began to focus. Despite being blind, she could tap into her powers to sense energy given off by living creatures. In one instance, she figured out how many guards were waiting for them beyond the door.

"Forty-two."

"Are you sure?"

"My bad I missed the warden. That's Forty-three. You think this will be a fair fight?"

"Not even close..."

"Yeah. I wish them good luck."

As they opened the prison door, they could see the warden charging in with his army behind him holding their weapons up high. Charlotte took a deep breath before storming towards her enemies with a sword she picked up earlier from one of the orcs. Her enemies thought they could overpower her but they were mistaken.

Suddenly, another Charlotte appeared and then another and then another. The warden and his army were so flustered by the sight of seeing multiple Charlottes that their movements were hindered giving Charlotte a greater edge in the fight.

In less than five minutes, the battle was nearly over. Forty-two orc soldiers were defeated, leaving only the warden remaining.

"Don't think you are so tough because you could handle my underlings. Unlike my low-ranking soldiers, I can see through your tricks. There isn't an army of you, those are only mirror images cast by your friend!"

Although he was correct, Charlotte didn't show any change in her expression. They faced off at opposite ends of the room and then charged at each other with their weapons in hand. When they met in the middle, Charlotte's sword had completely missed the target but the warden drove his giant scimitar right through Charlotte's chest.

He was in disbelief at first but then he became ecstatic when he thought he had defeated Charlotte. "Haha, I, the warden of this prison will be given a promotion by the Mad King! Not only that, I will be famous and known throughout the land for slaying the treacherous Charlotte!" After bragging, he realized he still had to take care of Seert, but as he turned around to find her, he saw the blind seer with a smile on her face.

He was confused as to why she was smiling so he turned around to make sure Charlotte's body was still there but when he looked the body had disappeared. The Charlotte that he struck was only an illusion. The instant he discovered that fact, Charlotte performed two slashes in quick succession and the warden fell to the ground.

After the battle, Charlotte threw away the sword and walked away from her enemy. Seert was about to follow closely behind but she decided to visit the warden first. She waved goodbye to the warden, who was in disbelief because what seemed impossible before was happening before his eyes. Seert, The All Seeing Seer was now free.

Town of Anjen

The trio of Bella, Nathan, and Chelsea along with their dragon, Leeloo, were entering the town of Anjen. They had been travelling for quite some time and were looking for a nice place to relax and get some food. They happened to stumble upon a tavern known as Alno's Tavern where they would take a table for four.

A female server came around to their table shortly after they arrived to take their order. Bella gave her order first then Chelsea went after, asking what food they had that would be most satisfying for Leeloo. The waitress shared her thoughts and then wrote down their orders before turning to Nathan. But nothing could prepare for what he was about to say.

"I'll have four large pizzas."

"Pardon me but could you repeat that sir?"

"Yeah, you heard me. Four large pizzas." Nathan repeated.

"So that will be shared among the four of you?"

"Nope, they are all for me."

With her eyes wide open, she wrote down the order and then disappeared to the kitchen. She wasn't the only one who was surprised as both Bella and Chelsea had their jaws dropped by the amount of food that Nathan had just ordered.

"There is no way that's possible. You will not finish all that food." Chelsea declared.

"Oh it's possible and you will see once the pizza arrives!" Nathan exclaimed.

"But where does all that food go...?" Bella questioned.

"Hey! I'm a growing boy! I'm..."

Before Nathan could finish his sentence, a little man with messy hair appeared before them who seemed to have little care for manners.

"Uhhhh, can we help you?" Nathan asked.

"Perhaps! I was wondering about that little critter over there."

"You mean Leeloo, our pet dragon?" Bella asked.

"Yes yes! Could you please tell me how much you would be willing to trade for such a fine specimen of science!"

Immediately Chelsea had her guard up and held Leeloo closer to protect her. "She is not for sale. Go away."

"How rude! It appears you need to be taught some manners!"

It seemed like there was going to brawl inside the tavern but before anything could escalate, the female server from earlier rushed in to interrupt what was happening.

"Excuse me, sir, you are scaring my customers and I'm going to have to ask you to leave. You know better as this isn't the first time you have done this..."

All of a sudden the man covered his face and began to cry. Nathan, Bella, and Chelsea were confused and didn't know what to do but the waitress just stood there with her arms crossed as if she had seen this many times before.

"WAH! Why is everyone so mean to me!? I didn't do anything wrong and now you are trying to kick me out for no reason!"

The attention of the entire tavern was suddenly on him. He was trying to make the waitress feel bad for her actions but the situation backfired when he heard a shout from the crowd. "Hey! I recognize you! You blew up my shop the other day!" Then another voice was heard. "Yeah! He did that to my store last week!" More voices began shouting out against the man.

Now that the tables had turned, the man stopped pretending to cry. He told everyone not to be so serious as he started to do a weird dance like he was holding coconuts in his hand. The crowd was not amused by his antics and they continued to march towards him in anger. Seeing his dance wasn't calming down the mob, he eventually abandoned his dancing and ran out of the restaurant but the entire mob chased after him.

After the restaurant cleared out, the only ones left in the room were Chelsea, Bella, Nathan and the waitress. The server immediately turned to her customers to apologize for all that had happened and went to get their food. Shortly after, she returned with their orders. Nathan was drooling over the food, but Bella had some questions for the waitress.

"So who was the weirdo that got chased away?"

"Haha! You are calling someone else a weirdo?" Chelsea added.

The waitress shared how she was quite new to the town, having only worked at the tavern for a couple of weeks. However, she explained to them that the man who was bothering them was notorious for being the menace of the town. He enjoyed pulling pranks on everyone and stirring up concoctions that created multitudes of explosions, causing massive damage to the town. He became known as Alex, the Mad Scientist!

When the waitress finished, Bella turned to Chelsea. "Hey Chelsea, I know it sounds a bit far-fetched but do you think this Mad Scientist could be one of the four..."

"Psh what!? No way! There is no chance it could be him!"

"Well, guess there's only one way to find out!"

As Nathan picked up one of the pizzas in his hand and was so close to having his first bite, Bella pulled Nathan away and he dropped his pizza back on the table. "NOOOOOO!!!! MY PIZZA!!!!!" And they left the tavern to pursue the Mad Scientist.

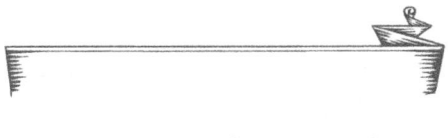

The Bodyguard

The angry mob pursued the mad scientist through the town. He tried to elude them by turning into an alley but was unfortunately met with a dead end. With the masses approaching close, he began to do a weird bird call out of desperation. The crowd was confused as nothing happened but they continued walking towards the scientist who scrambled to pull a concoction out of his hair.

Then jumping between the scientist and the angry mob, appeared a young squire with a peppy smile.

"Hi Everyone!" She greeted the crowd.

"Rianna you are late! I could have been badly hurt if you came any later!"

"Sorry, Alex... I kind of got lost."

"Well I have much work to do! I trust that you can take care of these crazy civilians?"

"Yes sir, you can count on me!"

After their conversation, Alex threw a vial onto the ground, causing a smokescreen to surround him. The crowd waited for the smoke to dissipate but when it cleared, the mad scientist had vanished. The mob tried to spread out and continue their search but standing in their way was the lone squire with a big smile on her face.

Bella, Chelsea and Leeloo were following the trail of the mob with decent speed while Nathan was lagging behind. They kept on going, hoping Nathan would eventually catch up but as they turned the corner into the alley they came to a halt. They could see the large mob with their backs turned, angry at someone in the distance.

Both Chelsea and Bella were worried about the mad scientist until they saw some of the angry people getting knocked into the air. Chelsea was kind of surprised because she didn't think the mad scientist was capable of defending himself. However, there were too many rioters for a single person to fight through so they had to act fast.

"Leeloo! I know you haven't done this before but this is now your chance. Go use your fire breath attack and blaze a path for us to rescue that crazy scientist!" Chelsea shouted with encouragement and the little dragon took in a deep breath and attempted to unleash a stream of flame from its mouth. Unfortunately, nothing but a couple of smoke puffs came out.

The little dragon felt like a failure but Chelsea embraced her in her arms and comforted her saying, "You did your best. We'll figure out another way." The only problem was they had no other options until Nathan turned the corner to join them.

"Finally caught up... so hungry. Need food!" Nathan was struggling to stand but when Bella saw him she immediately grabbed him by the arm.

"HEY! BELLA, WHAT DO YOU THINK YOU ARE DOING!?!?!" Nathan panics.

"We need a way to get to the mad scientist. Chelsea and I are going to give you a boost. You are our only chance!" Bella replied.

"WHAT!? NO BOOST NO BOOST! PUT ME DOWN!"

"Uhh Bella, I think he might have a point. This might not be the greatest idea..." Chelsea said hesitantly.

"You got any other ideas?"

"I guess not. Sorry Nathan but up to you go!"

"WHAT?!?! I WON'T FORGET THIS! I'LL GET YOU BOTH BACKKKKKKKKKKKK!" He shouted as he was flung over the mob.

The mob continued to charge at Rianna using groups of two or three but every time they would be defeated. They couldn't risk sending a larger group as they could have easily taken each other out. But their current tactics weren't working as Rianna continued to throw them aside, doing all this with a smile on her face.

However, over time, the crowd could see that Rianna was beginning to sweat and that she would eventually tire out. They continued to press the attack until they heard some random yelling from a boy being thrown over their heads. It was Nathan who was going quite fast and he was going to slam into Rianna.

Luckily, Rianna saw the flying boy in time and she managed to evade the collision but because of how unexpected it was, she let out a massive scream that would tear apart the entire mob's eardrums. The populace heard her deafening scream and they all scattered away. The only ones who stuck around were Bella, Chelsea, Leeloo and Nathan who was lying on the ground near Rianna after being thrown.

Looking at her big smile and innocent face, it was hard to believe this girl took on the whole mob by herself. However, the scream they heard came from her.

"Hey! Are you people looking to capture the mad scientist? Because if you are..." Rianna was ready to fight some more but Bella spoke before that could happen.

"We are looking for him but not for the same reason as everyone else."

"Oh? And why are you looking for him?" Rianna asked.

"We are, uhh, um." Bella looked at Chelsea for a moment as she didn't know what to say. Chelsea didn't know what to say either so she just gave her an eye signal hoping it would be enough. "Friends. Yes, that's right, we are his new friends!" She wasn't very convincing.

"You are his new friends?" Rianna moved closer to Bella with a skeptical look.

"Yes totally. We met at Alno's tavern!"

"OH! I know that place! You must be telling the truth! Come, follow me! I'll take you to him right away!"

Bella and Chelsea looked at each other with shock. Did the squire believe that they were friends with the mad scientist? As they were contemplating it, Rianna already grabbed Nathan by the arm and was ready to pull him along.

"What are you waiting for? LET'S GO!" Rianna said in excitement.

Chelsea and Bella decided not to overthink it and began to follow the squire.

As the cheerful squire led the way while dragging Nathan along, Bella and Chelsea grew curious about her reasons for being in the area.

"So Rianna, what brings you to Anjen? Judging by the emblem on your armour you are a soldier from Fifthguard." Bella inquired.

"That is correct! I am a soldier of Fifthguard but I have been assigned here to Anjen to protect Alex the Mad Scientist!"

Chelsea was pretty familiar with most of the customs at Fifthguard. It was extremely rare for a soldier to be sent outside their domain. There was only one possible reason Chelsea could think of and so she decided to ask the question.

"Yes, Chelsea! The reason I got sent here is because I want to pursue my dream to become one of the royal guards! To become a royal guard you have to pass many rigorous physical tests."

Bella and Chelsea were quite impressed and it was clear from her bout against the mob that the physical training was no problem for Rianna.

"However, most of the council members objected to continuing the examination of me being a royal guard."

"How come? You are strong enough to take care of yourself and protect others! What are these dumb restrictions and rules?" Bella outed.

"A bunch of the council members said they didn't like the fact that my voice was too loud. They said that it would give away the element of surprise in crucial combat or missions and therefore I was not allowed to continue."

"But someone stepped in and vouched for you." Chelsea intervened.

"Yeah! That's exactly what happened! You are really smart Chelsea!"

"Well, I didn't survive this long at the Gladiator Games just based on physical strength." She boasted a little.

"The one person who stood up for me that day was none other than Admiral Samantha!"

Both Chelsea and Bella looked at each other thinking if Rianna was talking about the same Samantha who was now the Warden.

"Admiral Samantha asked the council members to reconsider. Though the members were quite adamant about their decision, Samantha brought up the fact that there was a Mad Scientist whom they needed to transport safely to Fifthguard. So she suggested that I would be sent as his bodyguard and if I succeeded I would be accepted as a royal guard! But still, the council members refused and Admiral Sam did something no one expected. She said she would be willing to put her rank of Admiral on the line for me to partake in the mission."

"So that's why she is now the warden! She got demoted because of those no-good higher-ups!" Chelsea said in anger.

"That's why I must become a royal guard! So Warden Sam can have her rightful title as Admiral again! I will not put her belief in me to waste! I will successfully protect Alex the Mad Scientist and bring him back to Fifthguard!"

The two girls admired the girl's strength and determination. It was at this time that Bella decided she had to be more honest with Rianna.

"Hey Rianna, you barely even know us and you are leading us to Alex. How do you know we aren't his enemies?" When those words came out of her mouth, Chelsea elbowed her, implying the message, "What are you thinking?"

"Haha don't worry about that. I know I might not look it but I can tell you are very different from the mob that attacked Alex. You are all good people!" Her comments made them feel joyful. "Besides, after what he has been through, he needs some friends who care."

Chelsea and Bella weren't sure what she was talking about but Rianna chose not to explain. She told them they were nearing where Alex was staying and that was when they finally heard Nathan, who had been dragged around, speak.

"Hungry, so hungry, please! Need food!"

"Alright alright Nathan, just hang on a bit longer. We'll get you some food after we meet up with the scientist."

Within a few more steps, they came to a stop where they saw a home isolated from the central part of town. "We are here."

The Mad Scientist

Upon opening the door, Alex could hear the sound of someone entering. "Finally Rianna, what kept you so long..." When he turned to see that Rianna was not alone, he was alarmed and immediately defensive. "Why did you bring strangers into my lair? You know better than that Rianna!"

"Wait, Alex! These people are not like everyone else you have encountered! They are good people!"

"Oh no no no no no! I, Alex the mad scientist will not fall for such lies! You have been deceived, Rianna. But have no fear, the greatest scientist in Diamondlot will break their spell!"

Alex began pulling random vials hidden within his messy hair and he began tossing them at his targets. Bella and Chelsea immediately took cover at opposite ends of the room while Leeloo flew away searching for cover. That left Nathan who was still barely able to move but Rianna grabbed a hold of him and as the chemical mixed to create an explosion, the two of them rolled out of the building, leaving the two girls against the mad scientist.

Bella tried to calm Alex down so she could reason with him but he would not listen. The only way he would consider stopping his aggression is if they handed over Leeloo to him. Chelsea rejected the idea but Bella continued to wonder why Alex was so hellbent on obtaining Leeloo.

After taking cover for a few moments, the barrage of vials came to a halt and Alex could not be heard. Bella slowly peaked out the wall and she found that the mad scientist was no longer there. She wondered where he could have gone but she looked around and realized that Leeloo was missing. Chelsea jumped up and told her they had to hurry and find her.

They rushed through the room together but in their carelessness, they didn't pay attention to a hidden button under the tile of the floor. Bella stepped onto it, activating the trap door beneath her feet. Chelsea tried to grab Bella's hand but she was too late as Bella had fallen into the basement.

Chelsea was about to use the rope on her belt to help Bella but as the trap door was beginning to close, Bella told Chelsea to go after Leeloo. Chelsea didn't want to leave her behind but she trusted Bella's judgement and abilities. So Chelsea went on ahead after Alex while the trap door closed, leaving Bella alone in the mysterious basement.

It was extremely dark in the basement but thankfully, Bella had a decent scan of the room before the door closed, so she was able to pinpoint where the light switch was. After using her instincts to guide her to the light, the room was lit up and it revealed that this area was the laboratory of the mad scientist.

The room looked exactly what you would expect from most science labs but what shocked Bella the most was the equipment she saw. It was all so normal. It was so strange, Bella thought that a mad scientist would have the most sophisticated gear and she expected gruesome specimens to fill the place, but none of that was there.

Instead what she found was a notebook with tons of loose paper sticking out. Bella went to open the book and read through the content. As she was reading through the notes, she heard a growling noise coming from within the lab. She pulled out the spear behind her back and demanded the creature to show itself. The creature that made the growl slowly revealed itself out in the open and Bella was appalled as to what she had witnessed.

Back in the upper level, Chelsea was sprinting through the area. She searched room after room, as fast as she could but there was no sign of Leeloo or the mad scientist anywhere. She was beginning to lose hope when she heard the cry of a baby dragon echo through the building. Chelsea followed the sound into the room from which it came from. There she found Alex the mad scientist, holding Leeloo in his clutches.

"Let go of her you monster!" Chelsea demanded as she drew her sword.

"Don't take another step! In my hand, I hold an extremely foul concoction! No human or creature has been able to handle such a toxic fume."

"Throw that flask at me if you dare. I'm not scared of your stupid potions."

Alex was impressed by the girl's bravery but he maintained his posture. "Haha! Who said that mixture was for you?"

At that moment Chelsea realized that the chemical was going to be used on Leeloo. "No! Don't you dare!"

"Now now, I'm a scientist with standards! I'm willing to spare your dragon from this mixture as long as you listen to my demands."

"What is it that you want?"

First, Alex demanded that Chelsea drop all her weapons which she slowly complied. But it was his second demand that had her in outrage.

"WHAT?!!? NO WAY! I AM NOT SAYING THAT!"

"Oh that's too bad I guess Leeloo will have to…"

"OK FINE!" Chelsea was swallowing her pride and with every ounce of her strength she tried to speak but thankfully, arriving just in time was Bella to interrupt.

Chelsea felt a sense of relief seeing Bella but Alex reminded them that the situation had not changed. He still had Leeloo as his hostage and demanded they do exactly as he said. But Bella refused to listen and slowly walked forward towards him.

"Hey? What are you doing? Don't you know I have your dragon friend as my hostage! Don't make me use this!" Alex said nervously.

"Bella stop, he's going to use that poison on Leeloo!" Chelsea urged.

"There is no poison," Bella claimed.

Chelsea was confused but when she saw the look on Alex's face, she realized Bella was right.

"Ha, clever girl. So how did you find out?"

"I fell into your laboratory and although I don't know much about dangerous chemicals I noticed that you didn't have any of those stashed in your lab."

Hearing what she had to say, Alex threw the flask right in front of her, releasing the fumes into the air. Chelsea immediately reacted, still thinking the fumes could be poisonous, but the fumes were not. Instead, it was the most horrific stench they ever smelt.

"UGH! What is this atrocious smell?" Chelsea asked.

"Muhahaha! This is my ultimate stink bomb! I told you no human or creature can handle this!" Alex said proudly as he put a gas mask on.

After the foul stench subsided, Chelsea was still trying to figure out what was going on so Bella continued. She revealed that when she was in the lab, she found a book filled with notes in it. All the notes she found related to animal experiments, specifically animal health. Initially, it made very little sense to Bella why Alex was so focused on this topic until she saw the creature that lived inside the lab.

"So you met Matcha, my dog," Alex revealed.

"WHAT!?! YOU HAVE A DOG?! I wouldn't have guessed from how you treated Lee..." Bella elbowed Chelsea to tell her to stop.

"Your dog, she's sick..." Bella stated.

"I know. She has been like this for quite some time."

"What happened?" Chelsea inquired. Alex took a deep breath before telling them the story.

Long ago, Alex lived with his parents, older sister, and his dog Matcha. They lived in a town similar to Anjen where they lived an honest life but one day a massive swarm of locusts invaded the town. Many people were driven insane by the countless bites of the vicious insects. Alex came close to experiencing the same fate but fortunately, Matcha heroically diverted the attention of locusts to her. Because of Matcha's efforts, Alex survived but the people of the town were all lost. All he could find was Matcha who was severely injured and extremely sick. It was from that day on, that Alex swore to himself that he would do everything in his power to find a cure for Matcha.

"That's why you wanted Leeloo isn't it?" Bella asked and she handed the notebook back.

Alex flipped to the page he wanted and nodded. "Through my research, I found that dragon blood is very unique and could possess healing properties if synthesized correctly. Of course, dragons are extremely rare these days because they are in danger of becoming extinct. So when I saw your dragon, I couldn't resist."

Suddenly, Chelsea had a different impression of Alex. She realized that his action was driven by his love for his dog. She could relate as she couldn't imagine what she would do if anything were to happen to Leeloo.

"I'm sorry I caused you all this trouble. Here is your dragon back." Alex held out Leeloo and allowed her to fly back to her friends. Chelsea gave the biggest hug to Leeloo as they had been reunited. They then shared eye contact for a moment and immediately, Chelsea knew what Leeloo was trying to say.

She walked up to Alex with Leeloo in her arms. "Here you go."

Alex was perplexed. "Why are you helping me?"

"It's called being nice. Thought someone as smart as you would know what that is."

"THANK YOU THANK YOU THANK YOU! YOUR KINDNESS WILL NOT GO UNREWARDED!"

As Alex was about to receive Leeloo into his hands, the power in the building suddenly went out. What was strange about the power outage was there were no heavy winds, storms, or natural means that could have caused it. Which meant someone or something knocked out the power.

The Bounty Hunter

After getting blown out of the house, Rianna picked herself up and dusted herself off. Luckily she hadn't sustained any serious injury and was ready to get back inside the house to find Bella and the others. However, before she could make her way back, she heard a noise coming from the town.

She turned her attention towards where the town was and she could hear people screaming. The people of Anjen were under attack by something and when Rianna got a clearer look, she noticed people running away from swarms of locusts. The people of the town were in trouble and eventually, it would make its way towards their direction.

Rianna knew she had to get back inside the house and warn Alex. But before she returned, she found Nathan still lying on the ground. She picked him back up and carried him back towards the house.

It was dark inside the room with only a bit of moonlight shining through the window. Alex was trying to make his way to activate the backup generators but little did he know, there was someone behind ready to strike him down. The person hid themselves very well but Bella just caught sight of the katana shining against the moonlight and she immediately drew her spear to block the attack, allowing Alex to escape the lethal strike. Bella had successfully foiled the assailant's first attempt but as they were still in the dark, Bella couldn't see her opponent who threw her hard against the ground.

"Bella! Where are you? What's going on?!" Chelsea yelled.

"There's someone else in this room! Don't worry about me! Protect Alex!" Bella replied.

But there was nothing Chelsea could do. She could hear Bella's voice but she couldn't see anything around her. That was when she heard the sound of Alex in peril. "NO! Please! I'm still so young! Leave me alone!"

Chelsea followed his voice and then she began swinging her arms wildly hoping to hit something. The person in the dark grabbed Chelsea's arm and then tossed her aside with ease. But thanks to Chelsea's distraction, Alex was able to escape for a few seconds which gave him just enough time to flick the switch of the backup generator, putting the lights in the room back on.

The light revealed a ninja within the room with their face completely concealed holding a katana, ready for battle.

"You two, stay out of this." The person had an extremely low and muffled voice. "This insane person who dares to call himself a scientist is my target."

With such a menacing voice, Alex ran behind Bella and Chelsea hoping they would protect him. Both of them asked if he had any idea who this person was. All Alex could tell them was that this person was most likely a bounty hunter sent to hunt him down. Bella and Chelsea assumed their defensive position and they weren't stepping out of the way.

"Hmph looks like you made your choice." Instantly after speaking to her opponent, she disappeared from their sight.

The two of them began looking around the entire room but they couldn't find their target. Then just outside the room, they heard someone shouting out to them.

"Alex! There's big trouble out in the town! They need your..." It was Rianna with Nathan on her back, shouting into the room. However, she couldn't finish what she wanted to say because as she appeared, the hidden ninja reappeared and grabbed Chelsea by the arm unexpectedly. Chelsea was then thrown with full force towards Rianna, and they were both sent smashing through into another room.

"Chelsea!" Bella cried out. She then called for Leeloo and told her to check on them to make sure they were alright. Leeloo was worried for Bella's safety but with some assurance from Bella, Leeloo quickly flew to check on Chelsea, Rianna, and Nathan.

The bounty hunter turned away from Bella, hoping she would be deterred from further helping Alex but that was not the case. Bella jumped on the back of the enemy and grabbed on tight. Unimpressed, the ninja grabbed her and then threw her against the wall of the room. Bella was now on her back and completely vulnerable to the katana that was about to strike her but Alex reappeared with a can of hairspray and a lit-up match. He was close enough to his opponent that when he pressed the hairspray the fire shot right at the assassin's mask.

"Are you seriously wasting your hairspray like that?" Bella yelled.

"What else would I use it for?" Alex asked in confusion.

"Well, that explains your messy hair situation."

After their little exchange, they looked back at their enemy whose mask had been burned off. They could now see the face of the opponent they were fighting but they were not prepared for who it was.

Beneath the mask, Bella saw the face of the server at Alno's Tavern but Alex knew her as someone else. "Annabelle? Is that you?"

"Whoa hold on! You know her?!"

"Both our mothers were best friends, so we were forced to be friends because of that."

"Well, this is one awkward reunion then…"

Alex shifted his focus to Annabelle and walked towards her. "Annabelle! It's me, Alex!" She slowly approached him from the other side of the room and as they got closer, Annabelle swung horizontally at Alex's head but luckily he ducked below in time and got a bit of a haircut.

Based on her expression, she was disappointed that she missed that attack but her eyes told everyone that she would not miss a second time. So the second swing appeared swiftly that Alex would not have time to evade but Bella was quick enough to block the attack with her spear.

"Whoa there! Aren't you two friends? Why are you still trying to hurt him?"

"As a bounty hunter, I am bound by my contract to ensure I complete my mission without fail."

"But he's your friend! Does that mean nothing to you!" Bella shouted.

"A bounty hunter does not let emotions get in the way of their mission." As she finished her sentence, she began to push Bella back. "Besides, I'm no friends with that traitor." She completely overpowered Bella and sent her flying against the wall.

"Traitor? What do you mean?" Alex asked.

She suddenly appeared in front of Alex and kicked him in the gut. "Don't play dumb, you are a mad genius after all." She then picked him up and threw him across the room.

Alex was badly hurt and Bella was not in much better shape to help. She could only watch as Annabelle walked up to Alex with her katana in her dominant hand. Alex attempted to talk to her but Annabelle's anger had clouded her judgement. She raised her blade in the air, dropping it down to where Alex was but the blade never made contact with the scientist.

Instead, a loyal dog appeared in front of her owner and let out a weak bark. Matcha was now standing between the katana and Alex but most importantly, Annabelle had completely halted her attack. She put her katana away and reached out with her hand to pet the dog.

Annabelle was happy to see Matcha again as it reminded her of her companion from years ago. Her dog, Cookie, was as loyal and caring as Matcha but after the swarm of locusts invaded her village, she was the only survivor left that day.

After what happened in her village, Annabella kept wondering, why did this have to happen to everyone and everything she cared about. Out of her rage, she forced herself to become strong to ensure nothing like this would ever happen again. Eventually that led her to the path of becoming a merciless bounty hunter. Over time, she heard rumours that Alex was still alive and causing trouble in the Town of Anjen.

She should have been happy to know someone else in her village survived but she wasn't aware of how much anger she still harboured in her heart. Instead, this whole time, Annabelle had blamed Alex, thinking he deserted the village to save himself. But after seeing Matcha and how Alex has been doing his best to take care of her, Annabelle's rage began to subside.

After her time with Matcha, Annabelle slowly made her way to Alex. She held her hand out attempting to help him up but Alex was still on the ground confused.

"This isn't some sort of trick is it?" He asked suspiciously.

"You have no idea how big of a bounty you have on you do you?"

"Wow, I didn't know I was such a popular guy!"

She rolled her eyes. "I'll spare you this time, but I can't promise I will be as generous next time we meet."

Alex still didn't realize how lucky he was to still be breathing but he was glad Annabelle seemed to have gotten over her rage. He reached out his hand so he could be helped out but as their hands were about to make contact, Bella sensed something targeting the two friends.

"Look out!" Bella yells as she jumps in front of them and intercepts a massive swarm of locusts that was heading their way. She took the lethal attack to the chest and was knocked out cold.

Annabelle and Alex were in shock with what they had just witnessed but they weren't prepared for what was about to appear next. A dark figure wearing a cape and had bugs hovering around him was staring at them with a menacing smile.

Swarm Lord

Within one of the rooms in the building, Leeloo was flying around hoping she would find Chelsea. She couldn't find them with her eyes but she heard some debris falling nearby and immediately flew to where the sound came from. When she arrived she found Rianna, Chelsea and Nathan covered in rubble. Leeloo flew down and began to help them out of their predicament.

As the rubble was getting removed, Rianna began to yell to Chelsea. "We have to get back to Alex now!"

"Yeah I know, there's some ninja person out for him so please calm down. And stop shouting near my ear!"

"No no not the ninja! There's something else far worse! We have to get there now or else everyone will be in real danger!"

Chelsea wasn't sure what Rianna was talking about but she had never seen Rianna so frightened before. She knew how strong Rianna was so for something to make her this scared, it must have been terrifying.

"If what you're saying is true, then we need to wake Nathan up if we hope to have any chance," Chelsea advised.

"But how are we going to do that?! This guy has been out of it since I met you!"

"Do you have any food?"

Realizing they were in the kitchen, Rianna went to the freezer and opened it. "There's a pizza in here! But it's frozen."

Chelsea then turned to Leeloo. "Alright Leeloo, this is your chance. Please use your fire breathing to heat this pizza so we can wake up Nathan."

After having failed them previously, Leeloo was filled with feelings of insignificance. But this time was different. This time Bella and the others were in danger and they needed her fire to wake Nathan up. She took a deep breath in and then let it out on the pizza.

Annabelle and Alex were on their knees against a terrifying foe who stood before them. They felt like they had met this being before but they couldn't pinpoint where. The ominous man motioned his hands and summoned a locust storm that surrounded the two friends.

The locusts moved at an incredible speed, so fast that when Annabelle attempted to charge through, her shoulder pad was torn apart and she received some nasty cuts. As the swarm continued moving around, their memories slowly came back to them.

"You... It was you who attacked our village!" Annabelle yelled.

"Hmm, I'm sorry but I have no recollection of who you are. After all, I'm the Swarm Lord, sent here by the Mad King to destroy this town and every inhabitant within it."

"Ha, you must be a low-ranking soldier because you clearly missed a few targets." Alex taunted.

The insult infuriated the Swarm Lord, causing the locust tornado that surrounded Alex and Annabelle to spin even faster. Not only that, the swarm was slowly inching closer to the two friends.

"I don't know who you two are but if you survived my army of locusts years ago, I won't make that same mistake twice. BEGONE!"

He was about to signal his insects to finish the job, but a wild human tornado came spinning in, forcing the Swarm Lord to evade the attack. The tornado then went straight at the swarm of locusts and smacked them all away. Once Annabelle and Alex were safe, the wind began to dissipate and Nathan appeared in front of them holding a giant sword.

After he saw that the two were okay, he turned his focus to the Swarm Lord. He let out a loud warcry and fought the Swarm Lord head-on. The Swarm Lord was more than ready to take on Nathan but what he didn't expect was Chelsea using her lasso to bind one of his arms, preventing him from commanding his horde of insects. That allowed Nathan to get the first strike against his opponent.

However, after that first attack, the Swarm Lord resummoned his insects, forcing Nathan back. The bugs also chewed the rope that Chelsea had used. This was going to be a tough battle as Leeloo flew in to help the two fighters as well.

With the Swarm Lord distracted Annabelle and Alex were given a bit of time to pick themselves up. Alex went to check on Annabelle knowing she sustained a wound from the locust storm. But while he was about to ask her, he heard a loud voice coming.

"Alex! Thank goodness you are still alive!"

"Yes Rianna I'm okay, I don't..."

"We gotta get you out of here now! Let's go! Go go go!"

"But what about everyone else who is fighting?" Alex wondered.

"I spoke with them earlier, they said they would distract the Swarm Lord for as long as possible to allow you to escape! Now come on, let's stop wasting time!"

Normally this would be a routine decision for Alex. He was used to being chased and leaving when things got too dangerous, but this time, he felt conflicted about running away while everyone fought. He got a look at Annabelle's injury and noticed that it wasn't just her shoulder but she could barely grip her katana on her dominant hand. Alex stood up and instead of walking away, he faced where the battle was taking place.

"Alex what are you doing?!"

"Running won't solve anything. I have a feeling even if we escape, we'll just run into this bozo or another one of the Mad King's lackeys in the future."

"But what can we do? That guy is way too powerful!"

"Don't worry! I'm a mad scientist and I already figured out a solution!"

Annabelle was about to pick up her sword to help Alex but a surge of pain radiated through her dominant hand and she dropped her weapon. Her injury was more severe than he initially anticipated. Seeing that, he asked a favour from Rianna.

"Rianna, stay here and keep her safe."

Rianna could feel the seriousness in his voice so she didn't disagree or speak back. Instead, she held her weapon close and made sure she stood by Annabelle's side while Alex made his way to help everyone else.

Back on the battlefield, the Swarm Lord was outnumbered three to one but he was not outclassed. He had Nathan on the defensive, blocking the barrage of locusts with his giant sword. Leeloo thought she saw an opportunity to strike so she unleashed a breath of fire towards the Swarm Lord but he somehow blocked the fiery blast.

The Swarm Lord then countered by completely overpowering Nathan's sword, sending him lying on his back. He followed it up by unleashing a torrent of locusts right at Leeloo but unselfishly, Chelsea jumped in front of her and took the attack full on.

The situation looked bleak. Nathan was breathing heavily on the ground and Chelsea had sustained a severe wound. Leeloo flew by Chelsea's side to try to help her up but she could not move. The Swarm Lord was in full control of the battle. He raised his arms, ready to command his army to finish the fight but Alex called for his attention.

"Oh, it's you again. I thought you would run away like a coward."

Alex had no reply, instead, he pulled out a flask that contained a concoction that he had just brewed. He threw it right at the Swarm Lord who broke the flask midair and the chemicals dispersed into fumes. It did not affect the Swarm Lord, who commanded another swarm to charge at Alex. The locusts tackled Alex repeatedly and eventually, he got hit so many times, that he fell to the ground but was still conscious.

With Alex lying on the ground, the Swarm Lord made his way towards him. When he got within inches of the scientist, something grabbed onto his leg preventing him from proceeding. Matcha was biting onto the Swarm Lord's leg, hoping to protect her owner.

"Mangy Mutt! Get off!" He struggled to shake off the loyal dog and eventually, he succeeded. However, he wasn't satisfied with just tossing Matcha aside, he wanted to further discipline the dog. He was about to command his locusts to bite the defensive dog but again he was interrupted, this time by the injured Annabelle.

"Another annoying pest. Haha, you must be a glutton for punishment. I already know you can't move your dominant arm. You are no threat to me. Now step aside! I have to teach that mutt some manners."

But Annabelle refused to move, so the Swarm Lord used his locust barrage attack. With the surge of insects heading for Annabelle and Matcha, she began to whirl her katana with incredible speed and repelled the full attack from her enemy.

The Swarm Lord couldn't believe what had just happened and before he could fully comprehend, Annabelle lunged forward with speed and swung her blade rapidly at him. Under normal circumstances, Annabelle shouldn't be able to swing the katana with such control on her off-hand but a mark began to appear on the top of her hand. It was the mark of the warrior and it was giving Annabelle the ability to wield her weapon with full mastery.

Nathan, Alex, Leeloo, and Matcha watched as Annabelle had the Swarm Lord on the defensive. It was something they never thought they would witness. After a few more exchanges between the two, Annabelle landed a roundhouse that sent the Swarm Lord quite the distance.

Now the Swarm Lord was furious. He couldn't handle being embarrassed by a human, so in his rage, he gathered all his strength to summon up the biggest storm of locusts he possibly could but when he clapped his hands to signal his minions, none of them came to his side.

He was dumbfounded as to why his army was no longer listening to his commands. But then he heard a small chuckle coming from the Mad Scientist. That was when it hit him, back when Alex threw the chemical at him that seemed to have no effect.

"You... YOU DID THIS!" He accused Alex.

Alex continued to smile. The concoction he made didn't affect the Swarm Lord directly but had an adverse effect on his locusts. It was a chemical that completely disrupted their senses and so the Swarm Lord no longer had any control of them.

His pride got the better of him as he couldn't stand being outsmarted by a human. He charged at Alex with only his fists but the mark on Annabelle's hand shone even more intensely. At that moment, Annabelle appeared before the Swarm Lord. In just one second, Annabelle landed three consecutive slashes on her enemy and her enemy dropped to the ground.

The Swarm Lord could see both Annabelle and Alex in his sight and he reached out his hand, hoping he would get one last chance. But his powers had faded and his body was withering away. He could only look in disbelief at the two survivors from a village he decimated years ago, who found a way to defeat him.

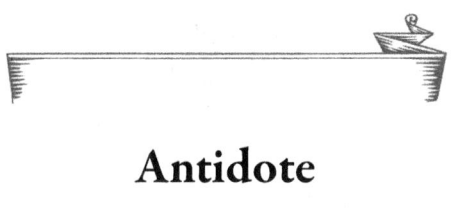

Antidote

With the defeat of the Swarm Lord, the mark on Annabelle's hand stopped glowing. Not only did she lose the ability to wield her weapon with her left hand, she became exhausted. She was falling towards the ground but Rianna caught her in time and carried her over to Alex. Matcha also made her way to her owner, licking his face.

Rianna had a sad look in her eyes as she saw the three of them had all been bitten by the Swarm Lord's locusts. Their skins were changing colour and whatever disease they had was slowly starting to spread.

"I'M SORRY ALEX! I WAS SUPPOSED TO BE YOUR BODYGUARD AND I COULDN'T PROTECT YOU AND EVERYONE!" Tears gushed out like water works out of her eyes as she shouted.

Alex weakly raised his hand and asked Rianna to move closer so he didn't have to use too much energy to speak. When Rianna got into whispering distance, Alex waited for the perfect moment and then surprised her by pulling out a vial containing a mysterious liquid. It was the antidote!

"WHAT IN THE WORLD? HOW DID YOU? WHEN?"

Alex told Rianna that he caught one of the locusts when the Swarm Lord attacked him. Then while the Swarm Lord was distracted by everyone else, he extracted the bug and turned it into the antidote. He said all this with a proud and somewhat smug face. Rianna was furious that Alex had her worried so she began smacking the mad scientist.

While that was going on, they heard something flying above their heads that was looking to land. They saw a griffin that had a rider on it and he was darting towards where Nathan was lying down. When the griffin landed, the rider immediately jumped off his mount.

"HAVE NO FEAR I'M HERE! WHERE ARE ALL THE BAD GUYS! BRING THEM ON BECAUSE SEBASTIAN IS READY TO RUMBLE!"

Sebastian looked around but he didn't see any enemies within sight. He was very confused so he asked Nathan, "Hey where are all the bad guys?"

"Uh, we beat them already. You are kind of late." Nathan replied.

"Haha! So they all ran away cowering in fear because they heard the great SEBASTIAN was approaching!"

Nathan smacked his face in disappointment. As Sebastian was still striking a hero pose, Leeloo was crying out for their attention. Sebastian did a quick assessment of both Nathan and Chelsea to see how they were doing.

"Oh my goodness! This is bad. Real bad! You are both infected and the disease is spreading! There is nothing to do but panic! PANIC I SAY!"

He was about to start running randomly in circles but before he could do so, Rianna appeared and smacked him on the head. She told him to calm down before handing him the antidote to Nathan and Chelsea.

Shortly after receiving the cure, Nathan felt much better and was back on his feet. In contrast, Chelsea still had other injuries from the battle and she needed extra medical attention. Sebastian let Nathan know that he would be able to take Chelsea back to Fifthguard to get the treatment she required.

As Sebastian was about to leave on his griffin with Chelsea, Alex came dashing in to stop him. Sebastian waited for Alex, who was requesting for Sebastian to take Annabelle back to Fifthguard for medical treatment as well. With a smile on his face, he agreed. They got Annabelle onto the griffin and they were on their way back to Fifthguard. That left Nathan who was standing with Alex and Rianna.

"So what are you going to do now?" Nathan asked.

"The Town of Anjen was hit hard by the Swarm Lord's invasion. I will stay around and help as many survivors as I can. And after that, I will meet you all at Fifthguard to join in your resistance against the Mad King."

"Are you sure you will be alright making it there?"

"Don't worry, I have a bodyguard!"

With some parting words, Alex and Rianna made their way down to the Town of Anjen. Nathan was now left with only Leeloo hovering beside him. He and Leeloo both looked at each other, thinking they had forgotten something extremely important. Then simultaneously they both remembered and Nathan began to shout. "BELLA!"

He remembered that Bella was struck with an attack similar to what Chelsea had sustained, which meant she needed extra medical attention along with the antidote. Alex hadn't gone far so he could easily catch up to him but Sebastian was probably a long way out by now.

Nathan was now full of worry and his first thought was to rush to where he remembered seeing Bella. When he ran to the place where he thought he would find her, she was no longer there. The level of panic was ever increasing but as he turned around, he smacked into someone he didn't notice was there. He was about to apologize to the person until he looked up to see who it was.

"Bella?"

"Yeah, that's me. Where have you been?"

"Where have I been? Where have you been!? I have been looking everywhere for you!" After speaking in outrage. He grabbed Bella's arm and attempted to drag her along.

"Uh... What are you doing?" Bella asked in confusion.

"We need to hurry! You have been bitten by the Swarm Lord's locusts and you are heavily injured! We need to get you to..." Before he finished speaking, he had the sudden realization that Bella was standing and talking to him as if she was completely fine. He was dumbfounded thinking he must be imagining things.

"Uh, Nathan? Can you let go of my arm?"

Nathan snapped out of his thoughts and let go of Bella's arm. Leeloo then flew into Bella's arms and gave her a big hug. She then began to make her way towards their next destination while Nathan was still standing in disbelief.

"Hey, you coming?"

Nathan then ran up to catch up with them.

"So what happened to Chelsea, Alex, Annabelle and Rianna? Where is everyone?!"

And along their way to the next destination, Nathan updated Bella on everything that had happened.

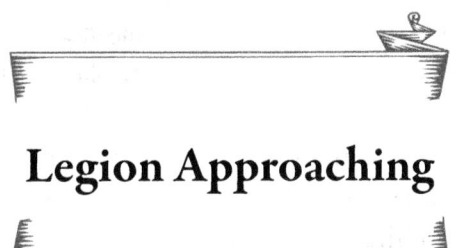

Legion Approaching

Within the Shadowlands, there was an area known as Skull Plateau where the army of the Mad King had gathered. There were masses of little goblins that were kept in check by the much larger orcs. Even larger than the orcs were ogres that towered over them. Some were even big enough to be the size of an elephant.

Then there were the creatures that came along with the soldiers. Some of them rode on vicious hyenas or flew on giant dark beetles. But even more terrifying were the Spectre Riders, dark knights of the Mad King's army that rode on flying serpents.

Hiding in the distance on an elevated platform were Charlotte and Seert. They picked off a small squad of the Mad King's minions and got intel that something was happening here. They were here to spy on their enemy to see what their next move was.

The Mad King's armies were squabbling amongst each other until one of the minions blew a giant horn that echoed through the whole plateau. Immediately, the entire area became silent, with the minions focusing on the center where the Mad King made his appearance.

Suddenly, Charlotte had an ill feeling in her stomach and although Seert couldn't see, she could sense an unsettling aura emanating not far away. They both watched from afar as the Mad King began to rally his troops. They remain silent to prevent drawing unnecessary attention.

"My loyal legion, the time has finally arrived for you to reclaim what is rightfully yours! Humans have infected this world for far too long. Let us take the fight to them! Today we march towards the final defense that remains from the human race. FIFTHGUARD!"

After he finished his speech, there was a massive uproar of cheers among his legion. The chants echoed through the entire plateau and they were raising their weapons in celebration.

Charlotte was filled with fear upon hearing the announcement. She thought they would have more time to prepare for the inevitable invasion but it appeared time was of the essence. Charlotte was about to tell Seert to send her messenger doves to Queen Victoria and Bella but Seert sensed someone was hiding nearby.

Seert pointed to a rock pillar where she felt the anomaly. Charlotte quietly smashed the pillar with her hands and hiding behind it was Kavan, the announcer from the Gladiator Games.

"Hi!" He waved awkwardly as Charlotte sighed.

"What are you doing here?"

"Well you see, after the Gladiator Games, there isn't too much happening around during this time. It gets very boring around Fifthguard so..."

"So you decided to follow me?" He nods as she sighs.

"Haha, sounds like you got yourself a paparazzi." Seert laughed.

While they were busy talking, they didn't notice a goblin patrol had spotted them. It made a weird screech, alerting Charlotte, Seert and Kavan's attention. Realizing it should have kept quiet, the goblin turned around and ran to find reinforcements.

Charlotte told Seert to quickly send the messenger doves while she took care of the runaway goblin. Kavan, not knowing what to do, asked if they needed his help.

"You just stand right here and stay quiet." Charlotte then chased after the little grunt.

The little goblin was quick but Charlotte was too experienced. She saw where her target was and threw a dart right at the goblin's neck. She hit the mark perfectly but before the goblin felt the effects of the tranquillizer, the goblin pulled out a stick and threw it in the air. The stick exploded, putting other minions on alert.

"Charlotte! They took the paparazzi guy!"

Kavan was getting carried away by an ogre on its shoulder. "HEY PUT ME DOWN! I'M WARNING YOU!" He shouted as he tried to punch the orc in the shoulder.

Charlotte was now chasing after the ogre but a team of four orcs blocked her way. They each had a weapon in hand, while Charlotte had her bare hands. The orcs thought they had an easy victim before them, but that proved to be their downfall.

They attacked her in pairs, with the first pair, getting ready to swing at her from both the left and the right side. Charlotte saw both their attacks and immediately did the splits and both the clubs just missed her nose. The orcs kept swinging their clubs and the momentum caused them to smack each other in the face. She then struck them both in the pressure point on their necks and took them both out.

The remaining two orcs charged at her from the front. Charlotte picked up one of the clubs from the ground and threw it at the feet of one of the charging enemies. By tripping one of the orcs, it fell and knocked out its comrade as well. She then took one of the swords from the fallen orcs and ran after Kavan.

The ogre had moved quite the distance but Charlotte already figured out what to do. She saw the ogre about to walk over a cliff full of unstable rocks. With the sword she stole, she flung it at the perfect spot of the cliff and the rockslide came rushing down toward the ogre.

Hearing the sound, the ogre stopped to see the landslide coming down towards it. Baffled, Seert swooped in and pulled Kavan away from the ogre. It happened at the perfect moment, just as she rescued Kavan, the rocks piled over the ogre.

"YEAH THAT'S RIGHT! TAKE THAT BIG UGLY!"

Seert couldn't believe how Kavan was acting but his attitude took a turn when a Spectre Rider appeared before them. Kavan was struck with fear from the sheer terror of the creature but Seert jumped in to use her ability. She threw a crystal up in the air and caused a massive flash of light but the rider and the giant flying serpent didn't seem fazed.

The serpent spat out a liquid that struck both Seert and Kavan which paralyzed their entire body. Charlotte, seeing that they were in trouble attempted to rush to their aid but multiple chains wrapped around her arms and legs and she too was subdued by the enemy.

After capturing the spies, a small group of the minions were feeling proud of their accomplishment. They were so full of pride that they decided to interrupt the Mad King's speech. The Mad King let them know, they better have a good reason.

Confidently, one of the orcs presented the three captives to the Mad King: Seert, Kavan, and the notorious Charlotte. The Mad King took a look at the prisoners and was not impressed with what he saw. The orc was confused until he looked at the prisoners again. When he took a second look, the prisoners had turned into giant rocks.

The orc's expression was suddenly filled with terror. He realized what was about to happen and begged the Mad King for mercy. The Mad King responded by giving him another chance and walking away. The orc thanked his honour repetitively, thinking he had been spared. But without even looking, the Mad King cast his dark magic upon the orc that had interrupted his speech. The rest of his army watched and then walked away as if nothing happened.

Meanwhile, sneaking out of the Skull Plateau were Charlotte, Kavan, and Seert. What happened was Seert cast her illusion magic that fooled the enemy's vision temporarily. Charlotte thanked Seert for saving their lives and they made their way back to Fifthguard.

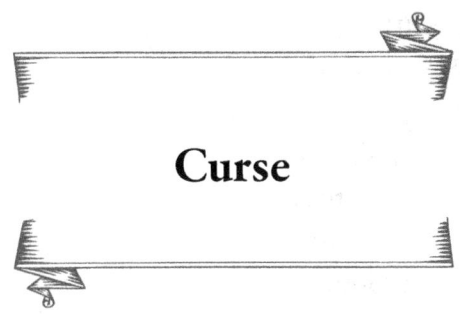

Curse

Nathan, Bella, and Leeloo were now out in the waters, having visited a dock near the Town of Anjen. The weather was bright and sunny, not a cloud in the sky but all they had seen was nothing but water for a couple weeks and they were beginning to run low on provisions. Everyone on board was growing weary and hungry, especially Leeloo who could barely fly at the moment.

"Hang in there Leeloo. I'm sure we will find land soon." Bella encouraged her.

"Hey! What about me?! I'm starving too!"

"Yeah, but you are always hungry."

"I can't help it. I'm a growing boy!"

Bella checked her satchel and pulled what was left inside. In her hand, she held some crumbs of bread that was barely enough for one person. Nathan was ready to jump all over the scraps but Bella immediately moved her hand away to allow Leeloo to take the rest. As he watched the dragon eat the remaining food, he asked Bella if there was anything left but there was none. Out of desperation, he reached for her satchel but Bella was trying to ward him away.

"Let me see! There might be some extra crumbs you missed!"

"No Nathan! Stop! Get a hold of yourself!"

While they were fighting over the satchel, they were completely oblivious to the weather that was changing. The sky began to be filled with dark clouds as a storm was approaching. Suddenly, a downpour of rainfall fell upon and heavy winds crashed against their boat and blew them out into the water.

Luckily they both knew how to swim and managed to keep their heads above water. However, the wind speed only continued to increase and a hurricane began to pull them in. Nathan, Bella and Leeloo were eventually caught in the hurricane. They were carried away with the winds and they would have very little recollection of what happened next.

When Bella woke up she found Nathan and Leeloo had already regained consciousness before her. She looked around to find that the hurricane had brought them to the shores of the island which was filled with sand. However, if they were to venture further into the island, there seemed to be a massive forest where they could easily get lost.

Without a sign of a watercraft on the shores, Nathan and Bella decided it would be best to explore the forest. However, Leeloo felt extremely uneasy about going into the forest. Her instinct kept telling her that something ominous was lurking inside and she also had the awful feeling that someone or something was watching them. But Bella and Nathan continued to walk forward and Leeloo had no choice but to follow them.

As they wandered further into the forest, they began to hear noises that were not reminiscent of any animal they were familiar with. Leeloo grew so concerned that she was no longer flying around but was now resting on Bella's shoulder, covering her eyes. They would continue to walk with their guard up when suddenly they heard a growling noise.

The noise completely startled Bella and made her jump into a fighting position. She pulled her spear out ready to fight but then she glanced over to where Nathan was standing who didn't have his weapon out. Instead, he had his hand placed on his stomach.

"Sorry about that. That noise came from my stomach." Nathan replied.

Bella and Leeloo were not impressed but another noise was made. "Nathan! I know you are hungry but would you please control your stomach!"

"Uhh, that wasn't me..." He replied nervously.

They slowly turned around, expecting to see a gigantic monstrous creature. But what they saw was a small creature waddling towards them. It had two feet, no arms, an angry-looking face and was green throughout. Most importantly, it was in the shape of a mushroom.

"What in the world is that thing..." Nathan asked as he stared at the awkward-looking creature.

The creature wasn't happy with his expression so it ran up to him and kicked him in the shins yelling, "GRECK!"

Nathan began holding his shin and hopping around to douse the pain. Meanwhile, Bella picked up the creature and shouted in excitement. "Oh my goodness! It's adorable!"

"You can't be serious... That thing is an abomination!" Nathan argued.

The greck gave a mean stare at Nathan. "Nathan! You can't just judge a book by its cover." She begins to hold it out in front of Nathan's face. "Come on! Give him a chance!"

"NO! GET THAT THING AWAY FROM ME!"

Nathan was running away but Bella kept chasing him with the creature in front of her. They ran through the forest with great speed until out of nowhere, someone in knight's armour riding a horse, thrusted his lance in front of Bella.

"Drop that monstrosity at once." Commanded the knight.

"Why is everyone so mean to this cute little guy?!?"

"That 'cute little guy' is cursed. If you hold on to it any longer, you too will be cursed and it will pass on to other creatures on this island."

"Curse? CURSE?! I DON'T WANT TO BE CURSED! Bella, we should listen to him!"

"What exactly is this curse called? And how do you know so much about it?" Bella asked suspiciously.

"This curse is known as 'The Greck.' This much I will tell you but if you wish to know more, you will heed my warning."

Bella looked at the greck one last time, before placing it on the ground to let it waddle away. After the creature had disappeared, the knight told them to follow him through the forest. He also instructed Nathan, Leeloo and Bella to keep their distance from one another to prevent the spreading of the curse. They complied and followed the knight and his steed.

Turtle Isle

After a short walk, they were led through a hidden path of a forest where they found a lake at the end of their destination. Bella and Nathan couldn't put it into precise words but they could feel that this was no ordinary lake. The knight pointed at them with his lance and signalled for them to get into the waters.

Bella and Nathan were still sceptical about jumping into a mysterious pool of water but Leeloo wasted no time. She dove in with glee and began splashing around in the lake. After seeing the jolly dragon swimming in the lake, Bella and Nathan decided the area was safe and they entered into the pool.

Upon entering the water, they felt peace and tranquillity, a feeling that they had long forgotten since the start of their journey. Not only was the lake cleansing their body from any irregularities, but they were also healing both physically and mentally. Bella was enjoying the peaceful moment but that wouldn't last long as Nathan quickly started making random noises and splashing the water profusely.

After they left the pool, they were greeted by the knight who had guided them there. The interesting thing was that his tone seemed completely different from how he presented himself before. He seemed a lot more welcoming and kind.

"My apologizes for how I spoke with you all earlier. My name is Zaid and I am the protector of this place known as the Turtle Isle."

"Turtle Isle?! I always wanted to go to Turtle Isle! I heard they have some cute turtles here but most importantly, I'm here to see the giant turtles! You know, the ones that you can ride on their backs! Please take me to them!" Nathan pleaded to Zaid.

"I'm sorry, the turtle population is in danger of going extinct..."

"What? But why...?" Nathan asked in disappointment.

Zaid couldn't find the words to explain, almost as if he didn't want to share. It was clear something was wrong with Turtle Isle and Bella had a feeling for the reason why.

"It has to do with the curse you mentioned before doesn't it?" Zaid nodded to confirm Bella's suspicion.

When I first arrived here, the island was thriving with both humans and turtles living together in harmony. This place seemed like the ideal utopia and many thought this would last forever. But one day a giant creature from the sea appeared and began devouring all the inhabitants of the island.

It would have destroyed the entire island but the 'Great Island Turtle' appeared and warded off the serpent-like sea creature. The people were saved but the 'Great Island Turtle' warned the people the sea monster would most definitely return.

The people initially had no fear as they had their great guardian to protect them, but little did they know, he was badly wounded. Over time the 'Great Island Turtle' grew weaker and nature on this island began to deteriorate as well.

That was when the curse appeared, turning turtles into these monstrous creatures. The people began fearing for their lives as this was an omen of worse things to come. So many have abandoned this island leaving it to rot to what it is today. I am most likely the only survivor left on this island, and I will do all I can to protect what is left.

The entire atmosphere had gone quiet for the moment. Normally this would be difficult for Nathan to handle but he understood some of the pain Zaid must have been going through. He looked at Bella and without saying a word, they both agreed on what their next course of action would be.

Nathan jumped up with a burst of energy. Then he told Zaid that he and Bella were going to help him get to the bottom of the curse and help save the Turtle Isles. Zaid felt a sense of relief as he had been on his own for quite some time. He had almost forgotten what it felt like to be in the company of others.

"Alright, everyone! Let's head out and break this Greck Curse!" He was about to lead the charge when Bella chimed in.

"Ok fearless leader, do you have any idea where we are going?"

Nathan immediately stopped where he was going and began scratching his head nervously. "I, eh, sort of have no idea haha."

Bella smacked her face in disappointment but Zaid appreciated Nathan's positivity and energy. The only problem was they were going to need more than a positive attitude to solve the mystery. It was at that moment that they turned their attention to Leeloo who seemed to have a lead for them. While they were having their conversation, Leeloo had picked up a scent and was flapping her wings as a sign for everyone to follow her.

So they gathered their belongings and accompanied by their new ally, Zaid, the three warriors proceeded to follow the young dragon.

Den of the Witch

Following the scent, Leeloo led the three into an area of the island that even Zaid was not familiar with. This area gave off an uneasy vibe and it did not help that the sun was beginning to set. They continued further until they came upon a den that had torches within lighting the way. Whatever was lurking inside, was more than happy to invite them in.

"Mysterious creepy cave. Why did it have to be that? It could have been a nice creepy cottage in the middle of nowhere!" Nathan agonized.

"No way, the cottage would have been way scarier!" Bella argued.

While the two were arguing about which scenario would be more frightening, Zaid, who was still on his mount, entered into the caves without them knowing. It was only because Leeloo flew in to interrupt their squabbling did they finally recognized that Zaid had left them behind. Upon finding out, Bella immediately rushed into the caves hoping to catch up to Zaid.

"Hey! Don't leave me behind!" Nathan chased after Bella to catch up.

Bella ran as quickly as she could through all the twists and turns while taking a left when she came to a fork in the tunnel. Nathan who trailed behind, had lost sight of her and he came to a stop when they split between the paths. He looked at both paths hoping there would somehow be a clue to let him know which way Bella went. But while he was still struggling, Leeloo flew in behind and startled him.

"Ah!! Oh, Leeloo it's you! Thank goodness. We need to find Bella and Zaid! Quick use your sniffy sniffy nose to find them!"

Again Leeloo used her nose to track the scent but there was a foul stench running through inside the cavern. Because of that, Leeloo never caught Bella's scent and instead, she just picked a random path, hoping it would lead her back to Bella. Nathan, not knowing this, followed Leeloo.

While Bella was alone, she continued running until she tripped over the uneven ground inside the den. When she picked herself up, she heard a noise coming not too far away. She cautiously approached the area as quietly as she could to see what was making that sound.

She arrived on the upper edge of a cliff and as she peeked down below, she saw a dark figure, holding a skull staff, exuding a similar aura as the Swarm Lord they faced back in the Town of Anjen. The unknown being seemed to be performing some type of ritual with his chanting. Circles with mysterious writing were beginning to light up as something emerged from a large pool of water within the caves. A roar could be heard from where Bella hid and she had a feeling she knew what was lurking within those waters.

"I got to go tell Zaid!" She spoke to herself. However, as she turned around, she suddenly felt an attack of dizziness. Holding her head with one hand and the wall of the den with the other, she tried to keep moving but the pain was too much and she fell unconscious. She had been struck with a dizzy spell and now she was about to be taken prisoner.

Meanwhile, Nathan was walking through the cavern with Leeloo flying near him. There was still no sign of Zaid or Bella so they continued along. As they were walking, Nathan was beginning to get hungry and he started to slow down. Leeloo, who was worried about Bella, encouraged him to move quickly but Nathan needed some time to rest.

When he was about to take a seat, they heard a noise coming from one end of the cave. It was a slow and low tone and it sounded like a creature groaning. Nathan had his hand ready to pull his sword and Leeloo was ready to pounce on whatever was about to approach them.

Suddenly they heard an abrupt screech that had Nathan jumping high up into the air. When he came back down he began running full speed away from where the roar came from. On the contrary, Leeloo wasn't frightened by the sound but she couldn't risk losing another member of their party so she flew after Nathan.

With his head down, Nathan continued to bolt down the cave hoping to get as far away as he could. Eventually, he was forced to stop as he collided against someone's back with his face. He held his head as he pulled himself up and although he was in pain, he was relieved to find the person he bumped into was Zaid.

He was about to shout out Zaid's name in excitement but Zaid covered his mouth before he could speak. Zaid made a sign for Nathan to remain silent and then he pointed in the direction of where he should direct his focus. Quietly, they peeked over the rock covers and saw someone who was communicating with the Grecks.

What they saw were four Grecks that sat down like an audience to watch a girl dressed in black, wearing a pointy hat casting spells. The girl was amazing, casting a variety of spells that involved: fire, ice, shapeshifting and conjuring items. When the girl finished her spectacle, the Grecks clapped their feet together and smiled as they applauded her.

"Thank you thank you! I know I am amazing. Please continue to shower me with your applause."

After she spoke, Zaid and Nathan looked at one another and gave each other a weird stare. They were both thinking that this girl had no shortage of confidence in herself. Then they returned their attention to the girl who had more to say.

"One day, I will leave this crummy den and show the rest of the world how spectacular I am!" As she spoke, she continued showing off her variety of spells. "And you, my loyal friends, will be with me every step of the way. I will reveal myself to the world and spread my awesomeness to the entire globe. MUAHAHHAHAAHAHAHHA!"

After hearing her monologue and everything she had to say, Zaid pieced together that this girl was behind the curse on the island. He revealed himself, leaving Nathan behind with Leeloo and confronted the lady on the stage.

"That's enough, foul witch! Your reign of dark magic is over. Stop your evil ways and I will consider giving you swift punishment."

"Who is this tin can man who dares interrupt my elegant performance, trespasses on my home, and calls me names?!"

"Tin can?! Revoke your words at once! I am a knight and not just any knight. I am known as Zaid the Speed Knight! No evil can outrun me, puny brat!"

"That's it! I will not take any more of your insults within my home. Prepare to witness the greatest sorcery in the history of the world. Don't blink because it will be the last thing you will ever see..."

With her last threatening remark, Zaid called for his horse and as he hopped on, he pulled out his lance, ready to fight the witch before him.

Truth

While the knight and the witch battled against each other, there was an audience watching from a distance. They were separated into two groups, one supporting Gia and the other supporting Zaid. On Gia's side was the small group of Grecks from earlier. Then there were just the two cheering for Zaid, Nathan and Leeloo.

The two sides kept their distance from each other while they watched and cheered for their fighter. Despite being beaten in numbers, Nathan and Leeloo would compensate through their sheer volume. To be honest, it was more Nathan than anything. He would be screaming at the top of his lungs, cheering for Zaid and Leeloo would just flutter around happily.

"COME ON ZAID! GIVE HER A LEFT AND A RIGHT! AIYEEEE!"

As Nathan got more excited, the Grecks on the other side grew competitive and began shouting back in retaliation from a distance. "GRECK, GRECK, GRECK!"

But the real conflict was happening on the battlefield between the speedy knight and the witch prodigy. Gia could cast very difficult spells without saying the full incantation. She could conjure poison darts, transform objects around her into sharp weapons and even levitate large stones. Every ability she had she threw them all at Zaid. Although Zaid didn't have a versatile arsenal, his armour was able to shield him from the ill effects of the poison darts and his mount was plenty fast, allowing him to avoid all the other attacks.

"You fight well, for a foul witch!"

"I don't need your backhanded compliment! I know my worth!"

"You are cold and heartless. Infecting the world and turning those poor turtles into those hideous monsters."

"I have no idea what you are talking about but I'm not going to let you talk badly about my precious audience!"

The two of them had enough of their verbal confrontation and were ready to resume their battle. "YES! LESS TALKING MORE FIGHTING!" Cheered Nathan in the background.

They reengaged in battle, fighting with all their might but as the conflict dragged on, Zaid was beginning to doubt. Gia's words and actions weren't matching up. Although she was fighting to defeat him, he couldn't sense any malicious intent within her. He was wondering if she was the person responsible for the dreaded curse on Turtle Isle.

As Zaid was lost in thought, Gia sensed her chance to strike. She cast a hex spell that struck Zaid's horse, turning it into a tiny frog. Without his steed, Zaid took a tumble onto the ground and he tried to pull himself back up. But Gia wouldn't give her opponent any chance to recover. She followed up her hex magic with a binding spell that had Zaid immobilized.

Nathan's jaw dropped in disbelief as he looked at the group of Grecks that were jumping in celebration and mocking him. With the cheers backing her up, Gia walked up to Zaid who lay on the ground defeated but not struggling to break free. She held out her hand that was infused with energy but she was hesitating to finish the speedy knight.

"Is the great and powerful witch of this den unable to finish her opponent?"

"Silence! I don't need you to tell me what to do!" Her hand was directed at Zaid but still, she wouldn't release her spell.

"You can't do it can you?"

"ARGH! I'LL SHOW YOU!"

"NO! ZAID!" Nathan yelled as the energy pulse came spiralling towards the defenseless knight. However, the attack landed just a few inches away from Zaid's face. The witch fell to her knees with tears flowing from her eyes.

"Why? If I could just hit you then I would be the greatest and the whole world would know who I am! So why can't I do it?!?!"

"Because that isn't who you truly are is it?" Zaid asked and his words struck Gia's heart and she began to reveal a bit about her past that she tried to forget.

Back when the Turtle Isles was still prospering, Gia lived with her family; her parents, older brother and younger sister. They all lived together alongside the small community of the island until one day the entire land began to shake.

Emerging out of the sea was a giant monstrous creature that resembled a sea snake. The beast's hunger was insatiable as it cleared out the entire human populace, leaving behind only one survivor, Gia.

With a measly child left, the leviathan began setting his eyes on the turtles. After devouring nearly eighty percent of the turtles, Gia's heart could no longer take the horror. A power that lay dormant within her began to surface which allowed her to save the turtles. She cast a spell that transformed the turtles into Grecks which deterred the colossal giant from eating them anymore.

Because of Gia's efforts, the remaining turtles were saved, but the spell was irreversible. Having lost all its food, the leviathan disappeared and was never seen on the island again. Ever since then, Gia thought she was the sole human survivor of the Turtle Isles.

After sharing her story, Gia released Zaid from her binding spell. He got up and held out his hand, offering to Gia who was shocked by the kind gesture.

"I'm sorry for accusing you earlier. You are a very kind person and I can't imagine what pain you must have endured losing so many people close to you. I too have lost many people I care about but I think there is a better solution than just trying to do everything by yourself."

"What are you suggesting?"

"We can work together." Gia was surprised by his answer. "It's something I learned from my friends Nathan and Bella. Although we had just met, they were willing to offer me their help without question. They helped open my eyes and my heart to become a greater person and because of that, I believe I can achieve more. I think this could also happen to you."

The walls that Gia had built were still strong but because of Zaid's kind words, they were beginning to crumble. She slowly raised her hands to accept Zaid's hand. Off to the side were Nathan and the four Grecks, still watching the events transpire. They were all starting to tear up over this wonderful new friendship. However, before their hands could make contact, a dark bolt shot passed Gia and struck near Zaid's chest.

Nathan and the Grecks were filled with disbelief as they saw the horrendous scene happen before their eyes. Thankfully, Gia managed to use her powers to catch Zaid, preventing him from falling back on his head. She slowly put him down to rest before turning around to find the one responsible for hurting Zaid. It was a dark figure wearing a warlock's robe and holding a skull staff.

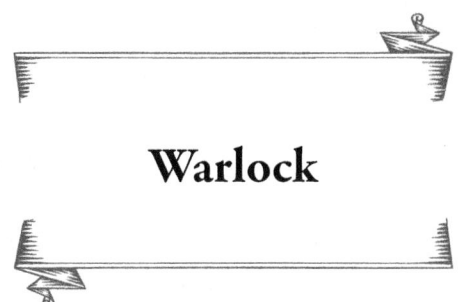

Warlock

"Hey I don't know who you think you are but you aren't welcome in my lair!"

Gia yelled at the warlock and then cast a spell which she hurled at the intruder. Unfortunately, the warlock reflected the energy blast with ease and sent it right back at Gia, knocking her down.

Leeloo and the Grecks saw this and were disgusted by what the warlock had done. With anger in their eyes, the critters charged at the warlock hoping to tackle him down. The warlock was unfazed and used his dark chain lightning attack to strike them all simultaneously.

The lightning was about to hit but Nathan was quick to act. He immediately pulled out his giant sword, jumped in front of the attack and spun as fast as he could in hopes of deflecting the attack. Unfortunately, there was no way he could spin faster than lightning so he took a massive hit and slammed against the wall.

Seeing what Nathan did for them, the Grecks and Leeloo reengaged against the warlock but he cast another spell that easily blew them away. They were all piled up and unable to move which left Gia the only one who was conscious but struggling to get back on her feet.

She managed to get on her elbows with the warlock slowly approaching her but she could not muster up any more strength to get up.

"It appears you have forgotten about me. Let me jog your memory." He tapped the bottom of the skull staff against the ground and behind was a portal that slowly opened. Inside was the sight of a slumbering leviathan that Gia was hoping she would never see again.

"You... YOU ARE THE ONE RESPONSIBLE FOR EVERYTHING!" As she suddenly found some strength to retaliate, the warlock cast a curse to weaken her.

"Annoying little witch aren't you? I should be the one who's infuriated with your presence."

"Can't handle my awesomeness? Well just wait, when I get my energy back I'll wipe the floor with you!" This time he was triggered and so he temporarily sealed her voice.

"Silence! You have no idea what you put me through! I was sent here by the Mad King to annihilate the Turtle Isles. It was supposed to be an easy task. I summoned the great leviathan by offering the island's inhabitants as sacrifices and then watching it terrorize your entire island. But somehow a little girl managed to save the population of the turtles by using a curse to turn them all into those hideous creatures! The leviathan was so disgusted by their mere appearance that it would not eat them and eventually fell into a deep slumber without any food.

Because of you, I couldn't destroy this island! Word spread to the entire Mad King's army, my reputation was sullied, and worse of all, I lost my ranking among the elites."

"Wow, you have some serious issues." Gia's resistance allowed her to break free of the cursed silence quicker than he expected.

"Enough! I'll put an end to your annoyance!" The warlock cast a spell that restricted Gia from moving freely. Slowly, he used the telekinetic spell to move her towards the slumbering leviathan.

"How disappointing? I thought with time you would have gotten stronger. That is why I disappeared for so long, preparing to face you again. Oh well, I'll have my revenge and the leviathan will awaken!"

Gia came inches away from becoming the last sacrifice required to resummon the beast, but a spinning tornado of lightning charged right at the warlock. He was forced to release Gia from his bind, dropping her just shy of the portal. The warlock looked as the tornado slowly stopped spinning and emerging from the electrifying whirlwind was Nathan.

"How?! You took a direct hit from my cursed lightning!"

Nathan showed his giant blade to his enemy. His weapon was now surging with electrical energy. "It was a risky move but I was able to absorb your spell with my sword. Thanks for upgrading my weapon!"

The warlock was slightly impressed but he wasn't going to hold back any longer. He raised his staff high and somehow conjured up a multitude of lighting bolts that were raining down on Nathan. This forced Nathan to use his whirlwind technique to defend himself. If he were to stop for even a second, one of the bolts would surely strike him.

The lightning continued to pour on against Nathan, preventing him from switching to the offensive but the warlock had been so distracted by Nathan he didn't see Gia hit him with a spell from behind.

Regretting his decision to leave Gia alone, he immediately launched a spear of dark energy right at her. But once again, Nathan spun in to intercept and deflect the attack away. They manage to keep up this pattern of Gia attacking and Nathan defending, which eventually drives the warlock into deep frustration. Because of that, he made more mistakes and got hit by Gia's attack, forcing him to kneel on the ground.

Seeing the warlock in a weakened state, Gia let up her attack but Nathan remained vigilant incase he had another trick up his sleeves.

"That's all you got? I expected more from a challenge from one of the elites. Oh my apologizes, one of the former elites of the Mad King!" Gia taunted.

The warlock was in no mood for games. He responded by casting a quick spell to create some separation between him and his two opponents. Then he cast another spell where he opened up a portal from the ground and pulled a person from below.

"BELLA!" Nathan yelled as he saw his friend in the clutches of his enemy.

"What do you plan to do with her?" Gia asked in a stern tone.

"Heh, I was hoping to have you as the final sacrifice but I always carry a bit of insurance just in case."

"No, you wouldn't! Let Bella go!"

"You are disgusting." Gia gave a death glare.

"HAHAHA! Say goodbye to your friend and be prepared to welcome the return of the great leviathan!"

As he was about to throw Bella as a sacrifice, a lance pierced into his arm. Bella was saved from being thrown into the portal and the warlock held his dominant hand in pain. Zaid managed to surprise the enemy at the perfect time even though he was barely able to stand.

Not wanting his efforts to go to waste, Gia used her magic to take control of Bell and move her to safety. But when the warlock saw what was happening, he used a reverse spell on Gia's telekinesis and without knowing, Gia accidentally pushed Bella towards the portal.

Gia, Zaid, and Nathan's faces were all filled with terror. They couldn't believe what had just happened and the worst was still to come. The warlock raised his hands and laughed hysterically to celebrate his victory.

Everyone in the den waited but after an extended period, nothing happened. The leviathan continued to sleep, the portal was slowly closing and Bella shot out of the portal, and lay on the ground.

"WHAT?! How is this possible?! The leviathan should be awake! It only needed one body of a living human!"

While he was still in disbelief Nathan dashed in to kick the warlock, knocking him inches away from the leviathan's portal. He then picked up Bella and began carrying her to where Zaid was but the warlock refused to quit.

Even though he was on his belly, he was able to conjure a mystical chain that wrapped around Nathan's leg, causing him to trip. With him getting dragged back, Nathan made sure to toss Bella over to Zaid, who caught her but now Nathan was in trouble of being fed to the giant monster.

The warlock had a firm grip on Nathan's leg and there was no escape but luckily Gia still had enough energy to cast another magical blast. Not only did it break the warlock's grasp on Nathan but the attack also sent the warlock spiralling towards the leviathan. As the warlock got pulled in, the portal began to close and soon after it disappeared. Nathan, Bella, Gia, and Zaid had survived against one of the Mad King's strongest minions.

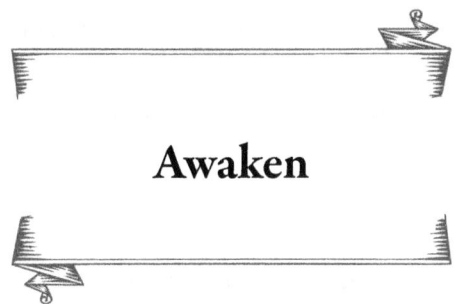

Awaken

After all the excitement had subsided, Bella finally regained consciousness as Leeloo was licking her face. She opened her eyes to see Nathan, Gia and Zaid all together.

"Uh hey, guys. Did I miss anything important?"

Zaid and Nathan looked at each other and tried to come out with the best way to simplify what happened so that Bella could understand. "Nope, absolutely nothing important!" They said simultaneously.

Bella then looked at Gia. "Hey, who is this? Is she friendly?"

Zaid and Nathan were about to respond but Gia jumped in. "How could you not know me?! I'm the great witch known as Gia!" She continued with her long introduction about herself but Zaid let Bella know that Gia was not their enemy.

With some of their strength regained, they made their way to check on the Grecks to see the extent of their injuries. As they were walking towards them, the ground suddenly began to shake. Bella immediately looked at Nathan, hoping that it was just his stomach growling but Nathan nervously shook his head.

They looked behind them to see the portal had reappeared and a giant snake-like creature within had its eyes open. The warlock that Gia pushed became the last sacrifice required and now the leviathan was breaking free.

Finding itself in such a confined space, the only interest the leviathan had was to escape the caverns. It ignored everyone and began slamming its way towards the exit.

Nathan and Bella immediately drew their weapons to go after the beast. Bella drove her spear towards the enemy but her attack had no effect. Nathan followed up by attempting to cut through its tough skin but his sword didn't even leave a scratch.

Zaid was still extremely weak and there was not much he could do. So he turned to Gia hoping for some answers.

"Gia, you stopped this thing before!"

"It was completely by pure luck. I didn't even know how I did it!"

"Nathan and Bella are fighting with every ounce of their strength! There has to be something we can do!"

"I'm sorry Zaid, There isn't a spell I know to stop this thing."

Meanwhile, Bella and Nathan continued their struggle against the monster that refused to give them its attention. They still attempted to hack away at the beast but it was all futile. Nathan was also so focused on attacking the creature that he didn't notice the collapsing rocks falling upon him. Thankfully Bella jumped in and pushed him aside from the rockslide.

As Nathan was thanking Bella for rescuing him, she began noticing her surroundings and figured out an idea to stop the leviathan from leaving the den. She rushed over to Zaid and Gia to relay her plan.

After tunnelling through the area, the leviathan had found the opening that led to the outside world. It was beginning to make its way towards freedom when Gia obstructed its path.

"Sorry big ugly, but you aren't leaving this place without my permission."

The leviathan let out a fierce roar but Gia was undeterred by it. When the colossal snake charged at the witch, Nathan and Bella began striking the walls of the caverns and rocks collapsed on their enemy. The leviathan was trying to move out of the way but Gia hurled rocks at it with her magic to keep its movement restraint.

Unfortunately, it was not enough as the monster began to lash out with its tail, knocking all three of the warriors aside. It looked as if there was no longer anything that could stop the leviathan from escaping but it took an unexpected fireball to the back of its head. Looking back it saw the tiny dragon that refused to let it leave, Leeloo.

Leeloo flew straight towards her gigantic foe. It stood still waiting to receive her attack but before Leeloo made contact, Gia had one last trick up her sleeve.

She cast a spell that made Leeloo grow until she was the size of an adult dragon. Not only was Leeloo larger but her strength was also amplified. It was with this new power that Leeloo tackled the Leviathan and was able to hold the colossal beast down.

"Now's our chance! Let's go!"

After hearing Gia's signal, Bella had Zaid's arm over her shoulder and they moved as quickly as they could towards the exit. Following behind them was Nathan, holding one of the injured Grecks in his arms with the other three following him.

For a moment it looked as if the plan was going to work but the leviathan let out an outburst of power that pushed Leeloo back against the wall. Then it swung its tail chaotically and the impact sent everyone falling onto the ground.

Zaid managed to get out despite his injuries but as he looked around he saw Nathan and Bella who were completely exhausted. The Grecks were unconscious and Gia was barely standing. All looked grim and hopeless but something within Zaid was stirring and the pain in his leg was disappearing.

"You got enough energy for one last spell?" Zaid asked as he stood determined beside Gia.

"You bet I do!"

"Good, save it for when I tell you. I'm going to save you all."

"Wait what? How are you..."

Before Gia could finish asking him, Zaid had moved away. Without his steed, his speed had somehow increased and he was now beside Leeloo. He made sure she was alright before asking her if she could hold out for a couple more minutes. Leeloo nodded her head and jumped back on her feet, ready to engage the leviathan one last time.

Again the Leviathan and Leeloo were locked against one another. Leeloo was doing her best to stall the fight as long as she could while Zaid rushed over to carry the Grecks out of the den one by one. He managed to save three before seeing Leeloo tossed aside again. Despite the situation, Zaid was determined to not leave the last Greck behind. He continued to run with fervor but the leviathan had its sight set on the speedy knight.

As Leeloo tried to get up again, she felt the hand of Bella who wanted to speak with her. "Let's fight him together this time. There's no way he'll stand a chance." Leeloo happily allowed Bella to hop on her back. Together they charged at the leviathan that was too focused on Zaid. With her lance out, they smashed into the beast and Bella caught it right in the eye!

This allowed Zaid to grab the last Greck and dash towards the exit. Once he was there, he shouted to give Gia the signal. In response, she used all her energy to blast the ceiling of the entrance so they could cave the leviathan in.

After Leeloo and Bella had successfully injured the colossal snake, they saw the ceiling falling apart which was their queue to leave. Leeloo began flying them out but when she got about halfway, her body shrunk back to her original size. Now she couldn't carry Bella, who had no strength left to run and to make matters worse, the leviathan was trying to catch them.

Nathan and Gia looked helplessly at the situation as they were both completely out of gas. There was nothing left they could do but Zaid refused to give in. His body suddenly began to heat up and glow, awakening a power that had been lying dormant. He tried to take one step but his speed had increased so much he dashed to Bella and Leeloo in mere seconds. With each of them in his arms, he dashed back out of the caverns as the leviathan missed his chance to attack.

Zaid had rescued everyone from the den as the ceiling fully collapsed, blocking off the exit and trapping the leviathan with it. Zaid then put down Leeloo and Bella safely on the ground. Everyone looked at Zaid who had a mark showing on his right arm where his armor was broken off. He was one of the four warriors that possessed the mark.

The Great Island Turtle

After having defeated their colossal foe, everyone finally fell to the ground completely exhausted. They had a big laugh together after the shared struggle they had. Everyone that seemed so different from one another had something in common.

"You are one of the warriors who possesses the mark of the legendary warrior," Bella stated.

"I guess so. Sorry, I kept that from you all." Zaid responded.

"I knew all along that he was the one!" Nathan bragged.

"Yeah right..." Bella was unconvinced.

"HEY! What about me?! I thought I was the one with special powers! Why does no one pay attention to me!" Gia yelled.

"So, what are we going to do about her?" Nathan whispered.

"Why are you asking me? You are the one who met her first. She's your problem!" Bella emphasized.

As Bella and Nathan continued to pass the responsibility of what to do with Gia, Zaid and Leeloo just looked at each other and shrugged their shoulders. It was quite a beautiful moment, but it wouldn't last as the entire island began to shake. All at once they looked back at the sealed den and breaking free from its prison was the leviathan.

Resurfacing back into the world, the leviathan was ready to dive into the open sea and wreak havoc on Diamondlot. Despite being at their wit's end, Nathan, Bella, Gia, Zaid, and Leeloo stood to face the beast once again. Unfortunately, the leviathan no longer saw them as a threat and blitz-passed them, knocking them aside without even trying.

After being cast aside, they watched as the leviathan reached the sea. They had the look of worry on their face, all except Zaid, who seemed calm. He told everyone not to worry but everyone looked at him as if he had lost his mind until the entire island shook again.

The true form of Turtle Isle was revealed as none other than the Great Island Turtle. With its appearance, the leviathan shifted its attention to its former adversary. The leviathan engaged its opponent but in seconds the Great Island Turtle had defeated the giant monstrosity by biting its neck and slamming it hard into the sea.

Because the leviathan wasn't originally from this world, its body quickly began to wither when it was finally defeated. It wouldn't be long before the remains of the leviathan scattered into the winds. The great threat had been eliminated.

The Great Island Turtle guided everyone onto his front leg so he could move everyone into a position where he could see them. Nathan, Bella, Gia, and Leeloo were awe-struck when they saw the sight of such a majestic beast.

"Oh my gosh! Bella, do you see it?! It's a giant turtle!" Nathan shouted in excitement.

"Uh, yeah. Kind of hard to miss it."

They continued to stare but Zaid assisted them in kneeling to pay respect to the noble animal.

"Speed knight Zaid! Thank you for your unwavering efforts in protecting the turtle isles. Because of your actions, this place has been saved and you should be honoured as a great hero." Zaid thanked the wise turtle for his words.

"Young witch Gia! By turning the remaining turtles on these isles into Greck, you have saved the population of turtles from going extinct. Your deed will never be forgotten." When he finished speaking, the Great Island Turtle placed its giant leg over the four injured Greck and not only healed them but reverted them back into little turtles.

Then the wise turtle turned to the remaining three that he had not spoken to yet. "Strangers, thank you for your efforts. Do not take what you have done here lightly. For none of this would be possible without your aid."

"Zaid, Gia, I believe both of your times here in the Isles are coming to an end. You have done more than your fair share and now your destiny awaits elsewhere. I assure you the turtles will return in greater numbers than before with the threat now eliminated." With one last thank you, the Island Turtle returned everyone on the island and then fell back into its deep slumber.

"So what do we do now?" Zaid asked but Gia was feeling much the same. Both of them had been on the island so long they had no idea what else they could do. The wise turtle didn't leave them with much information either.

"We could use your help in our fight against the Mad King," Bella explained more about their situation. How they had found two other warriors who also had a mark similar to Zaid's.

"I guess that is where we are needed," Zaid spoke out.

"Ha! You have nothing to worry about because you have the best person possible for your team! That crazy Mad King doesn't stand a chance with me around!"

"Guys we just have one problem. How are we going to get off this island?!" Nathan yelled.

They all looked clueless until they heard a noise coming from the sky. It wasn't a bird or some random flying object, but Sebastian was back on his griffin and he brought along a friend as they descended to the ground. It was Guranjan the shopkeeper.

"Have no fear, everyone! Sebastian is here! I'll save you from... Hey! Did I miss all the bad guys again!?" Both Nathan and Bella nodded with unimpressed expressions.

"Hey, Bella! Hey Nathan! It's been a while! I hope those items you bought from me a while back are helping you on your journey!" Nathan and Bella immediately went to Guranjan. They wanted to catch up with her and they were low on supplies and needed to restock.

After Bella and Nathan told her what they needed, Guranjan quickly grabbed her stash from the griffin and gave all the items that the duo requested. While this was going on, Sebastian agreed to help fly Zaid and Gia back to Fifthguard.

"Guranjan hurry up, everyone is ready and we are waiting for you!" Sebastian was getting a bit impatient but Guranjan let him know that she had one small matter to take care of.

"I know it's wrong to have favourite customers but I have a special item for the two of you!"

"Is it pizza?" Nathan asked.

"No."

"A new weapon?" Bella was hoping.

"Even better than both those combined!" Nathan and Bella were both confused as to what could have been better than food or an upgraded weapon. So Guranjan reached into her stash again and then held out a rolled-up scroll in her hand.

"Can I eat it?"

"Uh, what are we going to do with a piece of paper?"

Guranjan, still with a smile on her face, explained. "It's a town portal scroll, it... you know what, you two will be able to figure it out when you need to use it!" She hands it to Bella who, still not knowing what the scroll did, put it away.

After that, Guranjan began making her way to Sebastian meaning Bella and Nathan were about to head oppositely but something kept them from moving. Leeloo was just standing still with her head down, looking sad.

Bella walks up to Leeloo and pats her on the head. "You miss Chelsea don't you?" The dragon blinked to confirm what Bella was saying. She then looked over to Guranjan who was heading over to Sebastian, Zaid and Gia.

"Go with them. They will take you to where Chelsea is." Leeloo's eyes were wide open. She was extremely excited to hear those words from Bella but at the same time, she felt a mountain of sorrow for leaving another friend.

Bella assured Leeloo that she would be fine because she had Nathan watching her back. She also reminded Leeloo that she would return to see both her and Chelsea again in Fifthguard once they found the last marked warrior. Both Nathan and Bella watched as Sebastian commanded his trusted griffin to take off with Zaid, Gia, Guranjan and Leeloo.

Now that everyone else had left, Bella and Nathan had their sight set on finding the final warrior. There was only one problem they neglected. "Hey, Bella? How in the world are we going to get out of here?"

They looked around to find that there was nothing they could use to get off the island. The duo was completely stranded on the island without anyone to help, or so they thought.

Bursting out of the water was a large turtle that came to the surface of the water. It stopped near Bell and Nathan, welcoming them aboard. Before hopping on board, the two shouted thank you to the Great Island Turtle for sending them a transport turtle and with that, they were on their way to locate the final warrior.

Brawl in Fifthguard

Within her chambers, Queen Victoria looked out of her window where she saw a peaceful view of the city. Such a sight would keep her calm and serve as a reminder of what she was trying to protect. On her desk were piles of papers everywhere that would drive most people mad.

The burden on her shoulders was great but many would not know based on how well she hid it. What was causing her the greatest amount of stress was the division among the people of Fifthguard. Although she was the queen, many of the high council members did not agree with her methods. They thought she was too naive and far too kind. The members were so against the queen that there have been rumours about a coup to usurp the queen.

She closed her eyes, took a deep breath in and slowly exhaled to calm her nerves. As she reopened her eyes, she saw a messenger dove flying towards her. Queen Victoria opened her window to allow the flying bird into her room to land on her finger. After all she had to deal with, she was hoping for some good news, but as she stared into the eyes of the bird, she saw visions of what was heading toward Fifthguard.

When the visions ended, Victoria's consciousness returned but she fell onto the ground. Upon hearing a falling noise, Zoë immediately opened the door to find Victoria on the ground. She rushed to the queen to ask her what happened but Victoria had some grim words for Zoë.

"Their coming..."

Zoë knew what she was referring to. She assured Victoria that she would take care of all the necessary protocols and have everyone prepared.

Returning to the coliseum where the Gladiator Games were held, this place felt different. All the seats were vacant, but down at the arena, some of the soldiers of Fifthguard did their training here. Even some contestants could be spotted including Naaz and Rylin.

Each of them was training hard and minding their own business when suddenly, Naaz focused her energy on her gauntlet and pounded the ground. Her attack was so impactful, it scattered debris throughout the arena, hitting some of the other soldiers. Most of the soldiers were too frightened by Naaz to say anything but Rylin had no such fear.

"HEY! WHAT DO YOU THINK YOU ARE DOING?"

"Uh, training. What does it look like I'm doing?"

"You are splashing rocks everywhere and messing up my training regime."

"Hmmm, it appears I am in the wrong place."

"Huh? What are you talking about?" Rylin looked confused.

"I thought I was training in a coliseum full of strong warriors. But so far I've only encountered whiny babies."

"HEY WHO ARE YOU CALLING A WHINY BABY?!"

"I didn't call you anything. But you did just call yourself that just now."

"WHY YOU LITTLE... I'M NO BABY! I'M THE CHAMPION OF THE GLADIATOR GAMES!"

"Tch, yeah right. If Charlotte hadn't knocked me out during that contest, you would have been done for."

Their bickering was creating an immense amount of noise to the point that some people could not block out their voices. One such person was Jett who came roaring in.

"Both of you stop talking! It's impossible to concentrate with both of you being so annoying!"

Jett drew Naaz's attention who was not impressed. "Can it Jett. I'll deal with you after I'm done with this pip-squeak."

After she turned her attention back to Rylin, Jett began to fume in anger. He did not take kindly to being ignored and as his rage built up, his shadow began to grow. Eventually, the shadow beast that was lying dormant within him awoke once again.

"I will not be ignored!" said a low shadowy voice.

The mere sight of the shadow beast forced all the other soldiers who were training to run away. The only ones left were Rylin and Naaz who were still infuriated with one another. But instead of just standing and talking, Naaz pounded her fist together, ready to fight.

"Ha, I always did want a rematch of what happened at the arena." Naaz voiced confidently.

"I'm going to prove to you all that I'm the champion of the Gladiator Games!" Rylin boasted while swinging his Morningstar.

"Both of you! BE QUIET!" Roared Jett along with his shadow.

The three were about to leap into a battle royale against one another but one last person was entering the battlefield. Walking into the middle of the fray, a young lady with a paintbrush in her hands asked, "Hey what are you all doing?" But her words fell on deaf ears. All of them continued their assault as Ava was caught in the crossfire.

Moments later, Zoë made her way into the coliseum after hearing that Naaz, Rylin, and Jett were caught in a heated brawl. She rushed into the arena hoping she could break up the dispute. When she arrived, she couldn't believe what she was about to witness.

Lying down on the ground were Naaz, Rylin, and Jett. The only person conscious was Ava, sitting in the middle of the battlefield. Zoë was baffled as she wasn't sure how Ava was victorious let alone unharmed. She was about to ask Ava what happened but they were all starting to get up on their own.

Rylin, Naaz, and Jett were all still in a daze when Zoë approached them. She needed their undivided attention as she had a very important announcement to make but they were not listening to her. Zoë tried everything but they still ignored her so Ava stepped in.

"Guys I think you should listen to Zoë." When the three fighters heard her voice, they were instantly struck with fear.

"Sorry, Ava we didn't know you were still here! Whatever it is Zoë wants we will do!" The three of them said nervously.

Zoë was in disbelief, she whispered to Ava, asking her what she did to three of the strongest fighters in Fifthguard. With a huge smile on her face she simply replies, "Oh it's nothing, don't worry about it."

Zoë was still very curious as to what mysterious powers Ava had that could have frightened Rylin, Naaz, and Jett so much. But with more important matters to discuss, she turned her focus back to informing everyone that the Mad King's army was approaching and they needed to prepare.

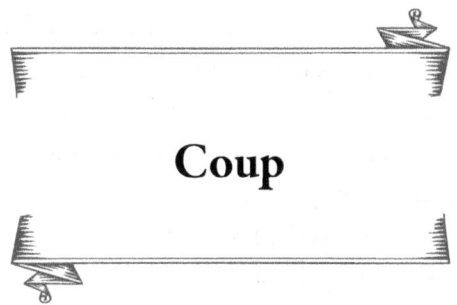

Coup

Later that night, while everyone was asleep, an elite assassin stealthy manoeuvred along the rooftops to avoid being seen by the night patrol guards. He successfully got through the entire bazaar area and even made it into the royal palace undetected.

Despite heightened security inside the castle grounds, the mercenary slipped through all obstacles, including the soldiers. He was now one room away from reaching his target, walking down a quiet dark corridor. Within an arm's reach was the door leading to Queen Victoria's chamber.

The door quietly slid open and the man slowly entered without making much of a sound. Having done this before, he found his target in the dark lying asleep on her bed. She was covered with a blanket, completely defenseless to what was about to happen.

The mercenary silently pulled out his blade and swung it at where the queen was resting. He struck right at where her heart was, but when the blade made contact, something didn't feel right. He flipped over the blanket to find that his blade pierced into a bundle of straw shaped like a human. It was a set-up, but it was too late for the mercenary to escape because descending from the ceiling was Annabelle, who locked the door.

Trapped in the room, the hired hand had no choice but to fight. He swung his blade, thinking Annabelle was an easy opponent because of her age. However, he was in for the shock of his life, as Annabelle easily blocked his attack.

"Sigh, you aren't very good are you? And I was hoping for a challenge."

The man was stunned as he wasn't expecting to battle someone of such an elite calibre. He threw some shurikens that Annabelle easily deflected away with her katana. That gave the hireling a chance to distance himself from Annabelle so he could break open a window to make his escape.

The mercenary was now running as fast as he could on the rooftops, but he wouldn't get far with Annabelle chasing in pursuit. Eventually, Annabelle was running right beside her opponent. The enemy took one swing in hopes of knocking her down but that was the last chance he had. Annabelle avoided the attack and then counterattacked by striking the pressure points on his body.

Once he was immobilized, she pulled out a rope and tied up the mercenary. He struggled as much as he could making it difficult for Annabelle to move him. So she knocked him on the back of his head with the hilt of his sword, making him unconscious.

When the man regained consciousness, he found himself restrained to a chair and his mouth covered. He tried to break free but the straps on the chair were too tight. He then heard a noise coming from a table counter not too far away. It was Alex who seemed to be handling some science equipment.

"Oh, you are awake! Just in time! I'm running a bit of an experiment and I need a volunteer."

The man was skeptical about Alex's tone and as he took a closer look at what equipment Alex had on the counter, he saw a full dissection set. Upon seeing those items, the man began struggling even more to break free.

"Oh haha, don't worry. I won't be using those on you. Who do you take me for, a crazy mad scientist? No no! I have something special for you!" Alex pulled out a syringe with a mysterious liquid inside.

"Hold still! You wouldn't want me to miss." Despite all the movement, Alex managed to inject the truth serum into the man's system. Once it took full effect, Alex asked the man a list of questions. Most about why he attacked Queen Victoria.

The next morning, all the high council members were summoned into the meeting room for an important meeting. All the higher ups were wondering why the meeting was called but they would soon find out. As they all sat around the table, Zoë barged in through the doors with confidence.

"What is the meaning of this Lady Zoë? It is extremely rude to enter into this meeting without special permission!" Dictated one of the council members.

"Oh, I have more than just permission. All of you are under arrest for treason against the queen."

All the council members stared at each other pretending to look puzzled. "Lady Zoë, those are rash claims you are making. The council will not take lightly what you have said."

"Well, I hope you all can take what I'm about to throw at you!" She dropped a massive amount of paper in front of all of them.

"Lady, what is the meaning of this?"

"These are all the evidence accumulated against all of you. All the illegal deals you have done behind the scenes, including hiring an assassin to take the queen's life."

"We have no idea what you are talking about…"

"Save it. Your hired henchman revealed everything to us. Not that he had much of a choice."

The majority of the council members were now filled with fear but the leader of them stood up. "Quite the annoying detective you are. I would consider you quite bright. But you don't seem to be the sharpest weapon on a rack. Coming here alone without any reinforcement was a huge mistake."

Zoë was outnumbered by all the council members and she had no soldiers with her. However, she continued to smile, which confused all her enemies.

"Heh, don't worry, I came prepared." As she finished her sentence, Naaz appeared in front of her, cracking her knuckles.

"How dare you insult us?! You think one girl can take us all down?!"

"I don't think so. I know so. Naaz, they're all yours."

"It would be my honour!"

Naaz took on all the council members and just as Zoë said, they didn't stand a chance. She made quick work of everyone in the room, injuring them enough that they were incapable of running away. And once she was finished, the soldiers of Fifthguard came in to arrest all the high council members and threw them in the dungeon. Finally, the war within Fifthguard had been dispelled, now they could focus on the greatest threat looming, the Mad King.

Double Trouble

After a long trip at sea on the back of a turtle, Bella and Nathan were immensely happy to be back on land. They were practically kissing the ground as they never thought they could miss the flat surface so much.

Once they had a chance to regain their composure, they looked around to see a place that was very different from the Turtle Isle. Instead of sand, this place was filled with wheat and scattered bushes throughout the area. Knowing time was of the essence, Bella and Nathan made their way to explore the plains.

After travelling some distance, their feet were beginning to feel sore. On top of that, both their stomachs were growling, Nathan's being louder. They were essentially out of food but they saw a nice rock not too far away that could be a good resting point.

When they arrived at the rock, they were ready to sit down and relax but they were in for a surprise. Jumping into position were two twin mages, one girl and one boy. They appeared before them and stood on the giant rock preparing to perform their motto.

"Halt! Stop where you are!"

"Don't think you can run away because we are the law!"

"All evil doers beware!"

"Thinking about picking a fight with us? It won't even be fair."

"I am, Vance!"

"And I am, Olivia!"

"Together, we are the Twin..."

"Dynamo!"

"Catastrophe!"

After they said their last words simultaneously, Olivia smacked her brother behind the head.

"Hey! What was that for Olivia?!"

"Vance! We agreed that we were the Twin Catastrophe!"

"But Dynamo is shorter and easier to remember!"

Bella and Nathan looked on as the twin mages continued to argue. They weren't sure what to say, so they waited for the proper moment to interject.

"OK Vance, we are going to try this again one more time!"

"What? But we have already recited it fifty... Sigh, never mind."

The twins were about to get back into their positions but as they were about to run their performance again, a giant ogre, holding a giant club in its hand, roared at them. It was unhappy that they had disrupted his nap and he was here to silence them.

"That ogre is going to smash those two to bits! We have to help them, Nathan!"

"I'm on it. Aaaaaiiiiieeeeeee!!!"

Nathan was rushing towards the ogre with his warcry but suddenly surrounding both him and Bella was a mob of goblins. They didn't look very difficult to handle but they were annoying and prevented them from helping the twins. Bella and Nathan wanted to engage in battle right away but something happened on the other side of the battlefield that drew everyone's attention away.

The ogre ran rampant, swinging its giant club above its head. It was loudly taunting the twin mages but for some reason, the little spell casters were not deterred. They gave one look at each other and the expression on their face had taken a turn. The silly-looking faces they had were now replaced with ones of focus and determination.

Whirling its weapon in the air, the ogre had its sights set on Vance. With great force, it attempted to pulverize the mage but the attack was completely nullified. The ogre looked confused as he stared at the unharmed mage who had been protected by a magical barrier. Then slowly, its dumbfounded expression changed into one of fear.

With the forcefield blocking the attack, Vance had a grin on his face and began casting a fire spell. Olivia lowered the shield spell at the perfect moment to allow Vance's fire spell to connect against the oversized grunt. The spell set the ogre ablaze and it began to fan the fire away on its head and bottom.

Once it put out the fire, it felt angry for being embarrassed, so he was ready to lash out at the little mage. However, when it looked back, it saw both the twins standing back to back, preparing for their dual-cast attack. Olivia casted a wind gust combining it with Vance's blizzard blast and the attack rained down on the ogre. After being pelted by the combination attack, it fled from the battlefield.

The goblins that had surrounded Nathan and Bella had witnessed what had happened with the ogre. Seeing their giant leader running away with fear, the minions scattered away leaving the two explorers alone.

Bella and Nathan were quite impressed. They weren't expecting the little twins to be so skilled in combat. As they were still staring at the twins who were arguing, Olivia turned over to speak with them.

"Anyways, what brings you two strangers into the Adenni Plains? I hate to say it but it ain't the greatest place to take a vacation."

"We are looking for someone," Bella replied.

"Oh, what a coincidence! We are looking for someone too! Well actually we are looking for a lost dog but..." But before Vance could continue, Olivia smacked him behind the head again.

"Owww! What was that for this time?"

"Vance! You aren't supposed to just go telling anyone what we are doing! We don't know who any of these people are! They could be intruders..."

"Hey I get it, we just arrived here and you have every right to not trust us. However, does this look like the face of someone who is a bad guy?" Nathan attempted to pull off a cute face with a smile but his face looked a bit awkward and got an eye raise from Olivia.

Unable to handle his facial expression any longer Bella grabs Nathan by the collar and pulls him away, hoping to avoid further embarrassment.

"Hey, Bella! What are you doing? Stop dragging me like this I do not approve."

Olivia couldn't believe what she was seeing. The two duo were completely ridiculous to the point that it couldn't have been fake. "Sigh, there's no way some silly goofs like you could possibly be part of any evil army. Follow me."

"Where are you going to take us?" Bella asked.

"The sun is coming down, it wouldn't be wise to hang around these plains during the night. I'll take you to where we are staying. We have a friend there who might be able to at least give you some food for the night." Olivia informed them.

"Did you say, FOOD!?!?" Nathan rushed to follow Olivia without a second's hesitation.

Bella shook her head but she couldn't ignore the rumble in her stomach. She was about to walk towards Nathan when she noticed that Vance was waiting for her to move first.

"Are you going to catch up to your sister?"

"That's okay. It will be much better if I stay in the rear."

"Why is that? Are you expecting something might happen?"

"As long as you don't try anything fishy, then there is nothing to worry about."

Vance finished that sentence with a slightly creepy smile. Although he wasn't very tall, Bella saw what the mage was capable of. She knew she wouldn't want to get on his bad side, so she turned away and followed after Olivia and Nathan.

Abducted

Further into the Adenni Plains, was a single cottage in the middle of the field. It was clear this area was once filled with animals and vegetation but how things have changed over the rule of the Mad King. Now, the only thing left were some wooden dummies with targets slapped onto them.

Standing in the distance from the wooden targets, was a hunter who held a recurve bow with a quiver filled with arrows. He took a deep breath while drawing the bow string and arrow back to concentrate on his next move. When he opened his eyes and released his breath, he didn't just fire one arrow but many others in quick succession. The speed at which he was able to launch the arrows was amazing but what was even scarier was how accurate the man was. Not only did he land an arrow on each dummy, but all of them were bullseyes.

After his training session was over, he walked up to one of the targets to reclaim one of his bolts. Upon pulling one of them out, he picked up an unfamiliar scent. Immediately, he put the arrow on his bow and fired it towards where the scent was coming from.

The arrow would have landed an accurate shot but it clanked off something, which made the man reach for another arrow. However, before more arrows could be retrieved, Olivia popped out of the bush and called for the hunter's attention.

"Rhyen! It's okay! It's just me and Vance! Oh, we also have some guests!"

Slowly, Nathan and Bella appeared out of the bushes along with Vance. They were all hiding to get a sneak peek of Rhyen's archery skills and they were not disappointed. When Rhyen caught a glimpse of Nathan, he saw the giant sword from which his arrow bounced off. Not a man of many words, he disappeared back into the cottage by himself.

"Nice guy," Nathan announced.

"He's been through a lot. Anyway, let's all go in! I'll get dinner ready."

While Olivia was preparing the food, everyone else waited at the table. There was nothing but awkward silence between the four. Rhyen had no interest in speaking with Bella or Nathan. Vance on the other hand was looking around avoiding eye contact.

"Almost ready! Vance, could you please come and help me!" Vance couldn't have got up any faster, as he hopped off his chair and made a dash for the kitchen.

Now the table had only Rhyen, Bella and Nathan. Unable to contain the dreaded silence, Nathan decided to speak up.

"So, where did you get that bow?"

"Nowhere."

"How did you get so accurate at shooting those arrows?"

"Training."

"You think you could teach me to..."

"No."

Having had enough of his attitude, Bella stood up in outrage. "Hey! My friend just wanted to be nice and ask you questions! What is your problem?"

Not wanting to reply, Rhyen stood up from his seat and walked away from the table. As he was doing so, Olivia and Vance were coming out with the food and he just walked past them to get outside and slammed the door shut. The twin mages pretended as if nothing happened and continued to place the food on the table for everyone to eat.

Nathan wasted no time once the food was all set and began to help himself to dinner. Bella and Vance were eating at normal speed while Olivia was setting some food aside for Rhyen when he returned. Bella couldn't shake off her first interaction with the guy so she had to ask.

"Hey Olivia I'm sure that guy is nice to you and your brother at times, but what is his deal?"

Olivia put down her food so she could collect her thoughts and share them with both Bella and Nathan. She explained how Rhyen used to have a pet companion, a cute tiny Maltipoo, that he had by his side at all times. She wasn't the most capable hunting dog in the world but for some reason, Rhyen cared for her. But one day, she suddenly went missing without a trace. Ever since that day, Rhyen has searched tirelessly for her but even to this day, he has yet to find her.

After hearing that story, Bella had a different impression of Rhyen. She wanted to ask more questions but she didn't know how much Olivia was willing to share. So instead of Bella speaking, Nathan jumped in.

"Can I have seconds?"

"Nathan!"

"What? I'm still hungry."

"Haha, it's quite alright. I somewhat expected you two to be big eaters. I'll be back with more." Olivia got up to get more food for Nathan.

After Olivia left the table, Bella's appetite had also suddenly disappeared. She put her food back on the table and left the cottage for some fresh air. That left just Nathan and Vance. The two were just sitting there but Vance had something he wanted to share.

"Hey, Nathan?"

"Yeah?"

"I once invited a friend over for dinner."

"Oh, that's very nice of you."

"He was delicious."

When he heard Vance's reply, Nathan's eyes widened and he felt a shock through his system. Luckily, Olivia overheard and rushed back out to smack Vance in the head.

"Owwww!"

"VANCE! Stop scaring our guests! You do this every time!"

Nathan moved a seat away from Vance, grabbed the food that Olivia got for him and continued eating. Meanwhile, outside the cottage, Bella sat down and looked up at the sky. She wasn't sure what it was but her head was starting to hurt and she was hoping some fresh air would help. So she lay down near the cottage and closed her eyes to get some rest.

When Bella reopened her eyes, she saw that the sky was now dark and the moon was out. She had somehow fallen asleep outside. She was about to pick herself up and return inside when she heard someone coming out of the cottage.

Although it was dark, Bella could tell the person who came out was Olivia. She was about to wave and call for her but she noticed that Olivia seemed to be acting a bit strange. Olivia closed the door quietly as if she was not wanting to get caught. After the door was silently shut, she made her way into the woodlands that were not too far from the cottage.

It seemed Olivia hadn't noticed Bella at all. And instead of just going back inside to sleep, Bella decided to follow the mage to see where she was off to in a rush.

Bella had been following Olivia's tracks into the woodlands and she found her hiding behind a thicket of bushes. She continued to stay low and silent until she was within arm's reach. Then she reached out her arm and tapped her on the shoulder.

Olivia was startled by the tap on her shoulder but she managed to keep herself from screaming. When she turned around she was glad to see that it was Bella behind her. Bella was filled with questions for Olivia but the mage held her finger in front of her mouth signalling Bella to remain silent. Then with the pointing finger in her other hand, she directed Bella's attention to what was happening beyond the bushes.

Bella took a look with her own eyes while staying hidden. She saw two figures speaking to one another. One was Rhyen but the other was someone she didn't recognize. She was a woman covered in a cloak with a giant scythe behind her back and she emitted a terrifying aura.

"As I was saying before, I have what you desire. I would be more than happy to return what is yours. For a fair trade of course."

"How do I know you aren't lying?"

"You don't, but are you going to pass up on this chance?"

Rhyen was struggling to come to a decision but Olivia had enough of just watching. She popped out from hiding to knock some sense into Rhyen.

"Rhyen don't listen to her! She's lying!"

"Olivia? Wait, don't..."

He tried to warn her but in an instant, the cloaked woman disappeared from everyone's vision. She then reappeared right behind Olivia and she knocked her out using her elbow.

"Ahh, this is one of the twins I heard reports about. This one must be the healer of the two. Explains why I took her out so easily."

Seeing her friend unconscious and in trouble, Bella roared out of hiding and pulled out her spear. The woman with the scythe saw her new opponent and attempted to use the same attack she dealt to Olivia. She appeared behind Bella but was shocked to find that she was ready to block her attack and retaliate.

"Hmmm? The scouting reports never mentioned anything about you. You are much quicker than that cleric over there."

"Ha, I know someone who's incredibly fast. Compared to him, you are almost as slow as a turtle."

Bella's comment had provoked the woman. Instead of wasting time to warm up, she cast a spectral chain that caught Bella off guard. It wrapped around her, preventing her from moving, which meant she was unable to defend herself. The woman swung down her scythe and a giant blade beam appeared and made a direct hit on Bella. She then fell to the ground, lying on her belly.

Rhyen looked at the situation and wasn't sure what to do. He saw that the woman was picking Olivia up and carrying her over her shoulder but she didn't seem that interested in Bella.

"Now, where were we?" She began to speak but then she stopped as she heard Bella beginning to move. "What? Impossible... No one has ever survived such an attack..."

The woman was perplexed and she began to move towards Bella. Rhyen suspected that the woman was about to land the finishing blow so he had to think fast. He fired an arrow that nicked the side of Bella's cheek but missed the rest of her body.

Bella touched the side of her cheek where she was struck and saw that she was bleeding a bit, but more importantly, she started to feel dizzy. Before collapsing on the side, she had one thing to say to Rhyen. "You coward..." And she lost consciousness.

The woman then called for her minions who were hiding in the surroundings and a few went to pick up Bella.

"Bring the boy with the giant sword. Once I have him, you can have your friend back."

That was the final message she left before her minions and she disappeared from their sight.

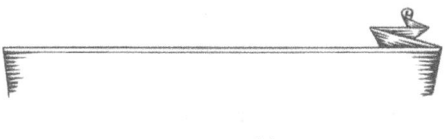

The Fallen

The sun was up and Vance had just opened his eyes but remained in his bunk bed. He had slept through the entire night without a single disturbance. He also thought it was quite strange that it was so quiet in the morning. Usually, his sister would be up nagging him to get out of bed.

He called for Olivia but there was no reply. After trying three times, he got out of bed and checked the top bunk. After climbing to the top, he found that the bed was all neat. No one had slept there for the entire night.

Vance rushed out of his room and down the stairs where he saw Nathan still sounded asleep. He placed his hands on his shoulders and began shaking him awake.

"Nathan Nathan! Get up!"

"Wahhhh! Aww man, I was having an amazing dream about pizza."

"Nathan, this is serious! I can't find my sister!"

"Alright calm down, we'll go find her. Let's wake Bella up and... wait where's Bella?"

Realizing that both Olivia and Bella were missing, they rushed outside. Neither of them was there and the two were panicking. They thought about which area to search for but they saw someone in the distance returning to the cottage. It was Rhyen.

He rushed back to tell them grave news that Olivia and Bella were in danger. That put Vance and Nathan on alert. They asked Rhyen what happened and where they were. He pointed them in the direction of the forest and they began heading that way immediately.

With their backs turned to Rhyen, he grabbed two arrows from his quiver and loaded his bow. Pulling them back, he then released them at the defenseless mage and warrior.

After quite some time, Olivia awoke from being knocked out and found herself locked into a cage. She saw Bella lying down unconscious in a cage across from her and tried to reach for her. However, her hands were tied behind her back with chains that prevented her from casting any magic. She struggled, hoping to break free but stopped when she heard an animal calling to her from a different cage.

When she looked on the other side, there was a much smaller cage and within it was a tiny dog that Olivia wasn't expecting to find. It was the dog that Rhyen had been searching for this whole time. "Biscuit!"

Her excitement was short-lived as the woman with the scythe had entered. "You monster! Let Biscuit go!"

The woman continued walking towards her as if she didn't hear what she said. When she arrived near Olivia's cage, she sat down. Olivia was confused and not sure how to react but the woman began to speak.

"You have a brother, correct?"

"Uhh, yeah. Why are you asking me that?"

"Tell me, what is it like having a brother?"

Sensing no ill intent from her, Olivia answered to the best of her ability. "Well, we don't always get along. Sometimes it's very frustrating because he doesn't do what I tell him." She paused for a moment before continuing. "But to be honest, I ain't the easiest person to deal with. I know he puts up with me and he is a very caring person. Life wouldn't be the same without him and no one could replace him as my brother!"

The brief story brought a genuine smile to the woman's face. Olivia was surprised as she wasn't expecting to feel emotions other than hate for her enemy.

"Your story reminds me so much about my little brother. I miss him." She began to stand up from her spot. "Thank you for sharing that with me. Tomorrow, your friend will return with the boy who wields the giant sword. Once I have him, I will let you and the little dog go."

"What about my friend, Bella?"

"She is an interesting specimen and I cannot give her back. I suggest once you are free, you leave with your brother and forget about her." She began to turn around to walk away.

"Wait! Before you go please tell me your name and what happened to your brother."

"My name is Kalea, the Fallen. As for what happened to my brother, it's none of your concern." And she disappeared from Olivia's sight.

Olivia then turned to Bella's cage. "Bella, please get up."

Within her head, Bella woke up in her dreams in a realm covered in mist. She shouted hoping someone would hear her, but the only thing that returned was the echo of her voice. Without a response, she walked aimlessly through the mist, hoping to escape.

After walking for what seemed like hours, Bella saw a silhouette of a person in the distance. Excited to see another human being, she rushed towards the silhouette in the mist. However, when she reached the person at the end, she was met with a surprise. The person was lying on the ground and not moving, but it wasn't just anyone. The person she saw lying on the ground was herself.

Bella was filled with confusion and shock. Her mind couldn't comprehend what was going on. She reached out her hand towards the body, looking to find a vital sign but she felt nothing.

"This can't be me... Can it?" She spoke to herself.

Then she heard the sound of water coming from behind her. She turned around to find that there was a pond in the middle of nowhere. Slowly, she made her way there and hovered her face over the body of water.

When she initially looked over the pond, she saw in the reflection the face of a man she didn't recognize. She thought she was hallucinating, so she shook her head and rubbed her eyes. Upon reopening them, she saw her own face on the reflection of the pool.

"What was that? Who was that? Am I just going crazy?"

That was when Bella began to hear another voice but it was faint. "Get up."

"Okay, I'm going crazy. I'm hearing voices!"

"GET UP!" This time the voice was louder and it got Bella to stop talking. "Your friends need you. Go!"

Those were the final words she heard as the world within her mind faded. And it wasn't before long that her body in the dream world vanished as well.

The Trade

The day of the trade had arrived. Kalea had both Olivia and Biscuit out of their cage but chained up. They were also heavily monitored by a couple of big ogres and a squad of goblins.

On the other side of the meeting place, Rhyen entered dragging two big nets with a person unconscious in each. One had Nathan and the other, Vance. He throws them both in front of Kalea.

"Here you are. Now give back what you promised."

Kalea pulled out her scythe and swung it swiftly. In a couple of quick slashes, she broke off the chains that were holding Olivia and Biscuit. Biscuit immediately ran to Rhyen who held the dog tight in his arms.

Olivia then looked at Kalea, who then cut off the net that encased Vance to set him free. "Take him. I only need the little one."

Although Olivia was happy to have her brother back, deep down in her heart, she knew this wasn't right. "No, I'm not leaving my friends behind. Give them back!"

"This is your final warning. Leave with your brother or else." Despite her warning, Olivia still refused to budge. "You are a fool..." Seeing that Olivia made her decision, Kalea no longer hesitated to swing her weapon. But she never got the chance because Vance woke up from his ruse with a serious look in his eyes and cast multiple fireballs right at Kalea.

The ogres saw their leader in trouble and were about to assist her but they failed to pay attention to Nathan who suddenly woke up and spun like a human tornado. He broke free from the net and reclaimed his giant sword to take the two ogres in succession.

The goblins all charged at Nathan but none of them came close to him as Rhyen drew his bow and fired arrows at a ridiculous speed and had the goblins running scared.

Meanwhile, Kalea was recovering her body after absorbing a few fiery attacks. She swung her scythe so quickly that Vance never had time to react but Olivia cast a shield spell over him. Thanks to her efforts, Vance was able to cast his lightning magic.

Kalea was able to block the first one but Olivia was able to cast a haste spell that allowed Vance to move and attack quicker than normal. He was throwing lightning quicker than Kalea could block them and eventually, she became overwhelmed. One of the bolts struck her near the chest, forcing her to drop motionless on the ground.

With their foe defeated, the look of seriousness left Vance's face. Right as he let out a sigh of relief, he received a massive hug from his sister.

"Vance you did it! You saved us all!"

"Olivia let go! You are suffocating me!"

As the two twins were reconnected, Rhyen stepped in to join the conversation.

"Oh come on Vance. You were so worried about your sister that you nearly burned me to a crisp."

"Rhyen! I knew you were on our side! But what happened?" Olivia asked in confusion.

Rhyen revealed the events that occurred the day before. Right as he was about to ambush Vance and Nathan from behind, Nathan sensed the arrow behind them in time and deflected them away with his sword. After he lost his chance, Nathan and Vance worked together and managed to overpower the incredible marksman. Nathan used his giant sword as a shield and gave Vance the opportunity he needed to cast a fire blast that knocked Rhyen on his back.

After suffering defeat, Rhyen revealed everything that had happened to Olivia and Bella. Vance was so enraged that he nearly incinerated Rhyen on the spot but Nathan stopped him from doing so. When his anger subsided, Vance was able to come up with a plan to trick Kalea. One where Rhyen would present Vance and Nathan as his captives.

"Aww Vance, you do care!"

"What? Rhyen doesn't know what he's talking about. He's gone crazy!"

It was a moment of happiness. The twins were reunited and the hunter had found his loyal companion after years of fruitless search. But there was still something that remained unresolved.

"Guys, Bella still isn't waking up," Nathan told them.

Everyone walked over to where she was and Olivia went to take a look. "She's still breathing and she doesn't have any injuries. I don't know what's wrong."

Biscuit began licking her face, hoping that it would help but her eyes remained closed. Biscuit made a sad puppy sound but Rhyen patted his companion on the head. "You did what you could Biscuit."

"Ummm. I might have an idea." All eyes were on Vance. "I heard electricity helps restart one's heart, maybe if I…"

Right as those words left his mouth, Olivia kicked him from behind. "VANCE! This is no time for your silly 'shocking jokes' or electrifying ideas!"

As they were busy figuring out the best approach to help Bella, they didn't notice what was happening behind them. A massive surge of energy was accumulating where Kalea was. The first one to notice was Biscuit, barking for all their attention.

"Biscuit? What's wrong?" Rhyen asked.

Immediately Biscuit hid behind Rhyen and everyone else looked in the opposite direction. They couldn't believe what was happening. They were certain Vance struck the finishing blow against their enemy. But a dark sphere of energy encased Kalea and everyone could feel something ominous was about to emerge.

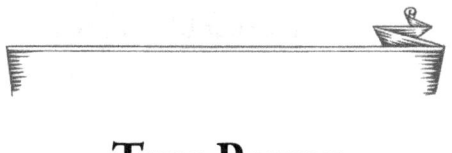

True Power

The dark sphere burst creating a huge explosion that blew everyone away. Materializing out from the abyss, was Kalea but she looked different from before. Her body was now plated with armour and the top half of her face was protected as well. And from her back, grew two black wings. This was her final form, that even the Mad King did not know about.

Olivia got up on her feet and she looked around to find that everyone was heavily injured. She then used a massive portion of her energy to cast a healing spell that would help everyone. Thanks to her efforts, Vance, Nathan and Rhyen were about to stand back up to fight.

The three boys stood on the frontlines waiting for their opponent to approach. Kalea took one look at their formation and easily assessed who her first target would be. She started by charging straight at them but the three warriors weren't ready for her next move. As they were about to simultaneously strike Kalea, she disappeared from their sight and reappeared in front of Olivia.

Olivia had no chance to react as Kalea placed her hand over the mage's shoulder and instantly she lost all strength from her body and collapsed.

"Olivia! You'll pay for harming my sister!" Vance was enraged and he left the formation.

"No Vance don't!" Nathan tried to warn him but it was too late.

Vance used every iteration of his strongest spell: fire, ice, and lightning. He threw everything he had at Kalea but with one swing of her scythe, she completely nullified the tri-attack. Vance was so stunned by her sheer strength that he froze, allowing Kalea to tap him on the shoulder and siphon his strength.

Rhyen had seen enough and wanted to take matters into his own hands, but Nathan continued to be the voice of reason. He knew the only chance they had against her was to work together but Rhyen would not listen. He attacked Kalea by firing an arrow to draw her attention but she swatted it away with her armored hand.

Her focus was now on Rhyen who she dashed towards with great speed. Rhyen stood his ground and fired his arrows in rapid succession but nothing affected Kalea.

Seeing Kalea distracted, Nathan attempted to attack her from the blindside using his whirlwind attack. He came crashing in against her scythe but again she was too much. She completely pushed back Nathan and sent him dragging across the ground.

With Nathan defeated, she turned back towards the archer. Rhyen knew this was his last stand and instead of running, he stood his ground. He was ready to accept his fate but something happened that he wasn't expecting. Biscuit jumped in front to take Kalea's lethal attack.

The expression on Rhyen's face changed when he saw his companion in trouble. He tried to reach out but there was no way he could make it in time. The scythe made contact against something but Biscuit was not harmed. Instead, Bella had appeared and she managed to hold off the swing of the scythe with her spear.

Kalea had been intrigued by Bella since their first encounter, as she had a hunch she was different from any other human she faced. Initially, she was planning to keep Bella to see if her instincts were correct. But since the situation had changed, she figured now would be the best time to test her theory.

She swung her weapon again, increasing her strength. Bella blocked the attack again but she was getting weaker by the moment. She refused to let Biscuit get injured so she had to remain on the defensive.

"You can't fight me and defend that dog forever. Sooner or later you will have to make a choice."

"I don't need to attack you. He will."

Rhyen was moving to a better spot where he would have a direct sight of Kalea's blind spot. He fired his arrow directly at Kalea's back but she knew it was coming. She waited for the right moment before disappearing and now the target of the arrow was heading straight for Biscuit.

Bella saw the arrow just in time and managed to shield the dog with her back, taking the arrow to her shoulder. Rhyen was relieved and grateful for

Bella's efforts but Kalea appeared behind him with a hand on his shoulder and siphoned his strength. She then turned her attention to the final fighter that remained.

"Your friends are all defeated. If you have any hidden powers as I suspect, you better reveal them now."

"I have no idea what you are talking about. But I don't need some cheap hidden powers to beat you,"

"Tough words." She then swung her scythe, creating a massive gust that blew Bella away, slamming her against a tree. "It appears you really have nothing left. A shame, I thought you could have been the one..." She reached out with her hand again to sap another victim's strength but when she placed her hand on Bella, nothing happened.

"What? How is this possible?"

While she was confused, Rhyen somehow arose after losing the majority of his energy to Kalea.

"Oh, it's you again? You should go back and lie down if you know what's best for you."

"You caused harm to my loyal companion, for that I will show you no mercy."

"Tsk, humans are so strange. Why do they lose their sense of reason over such small things? It's just a dog!"

Rhyen suddenly had an aura that overflowed with energy. Kalea had no idea but Rhyen used to have a younger sister who always played with Biscuit. Unfortunately because of the terror of the Mad King, many had disappeared from his village. The only thing left that reminded him of his family was Biscuit.

"You'll regret what you just said."

His arm was now glowing with a mark, signifying that he was the final warrior that Bella and Nathan were searching for. Rhyen pulled out his bow and in an instant, he fired a multitude of arrows at an inhumane speed with incredible precision. They were all on target and all made contact with Kalea, causing a giant smokescreen upon collision.

Bella, Nathan, Olivia, and Vance all witnessed the incredible display of power from Rhyen. They had never seen anything like it before but they were in for an even greater surprise. When the smoke had cleared, Kalea was somehow still standing, and her wounds were very minor.

"Heh, if that is your full power. You don't stand a chance."

"Don't worry. I'm only getting started."

While the two continued their battle, Bella and Nathan barely had any strength left to get up. Somehow, Olivia found the extra strength to get up and move towards Vance.

"Hey Vance, you awake?"

"Oh hey, Olivia. I guess I'm awake. That or I got hit too hard and I'm dreaming."

"Get up."

"What if I don't have the strength to do that?"

"You have enough energy to make your dumb jokes. Which means you can get up."

Vance knew from her tone that he should stop joking around. Olivia was very perceptive. She knew Rhyen had used up a majority of his power on his last attack. He would tire out before Kalea would. She looked to her brother and with just the look in her eyes, Vance knew exactly what they had to do.

Rhyen put up a good fight but Kalea's endurance and strength were too much. With his final burst of energy, he channelled everything into one final shot that struck Kalea's chest plating, causing a crack but no further damage. She pulled out the arrow and then knocked Rhyen down, ready to land the finishing strike.

"It was a shame you revealed your mark to me. I would have let you live, but because you are one of the warriors with the mark, I have no choice but to eliminate you."

Her scythe was raised but she held off her assault when she heard a couple of voices in the distance. She turned her head to find Olivia and Vance standing on a rock together.

"Halt! Stop where you are!"

"Don't think you can run away because we are the law!"

"All evil doers beware!"

"Thinking about picking a fight with us? It won't even be fair."

"I am, Vance!"

"And I am, Olivia!"

And together in unison, they said, "Together, we are the Twin... Dynamo-Catastrophe!"

They combined all their magical spells to unleash a massive magical blast that was aimed straight at Kalea. But she was not worried. Although the attack was more than powerful, she could see the attack slowly approaching and could easily move away.

She would have escaped but Nathan came whirling in and forced her to block his giant sword. "You annoying little runts! How many times do I have to knock you all down before…"

Nathan held on just long enough before jumping back to get away from the line of fire. He timed it perfectly so that a spear came flying in and pierced Kalea right in the chest. The same spot Rhyen cracked in her plating earlier. The damage was significant as it limited her movement. She looked to the person who threw the spear and it was none other than Bella. She then looked back at the twin mages' fusion attack that was heading straight for her. She realized this was true power, one where everyone worked together to defeat a common enemy.

"Heh, well done…"

The blast collided against Kalea causing a massive explosion within the area.

Past Kings And Queens

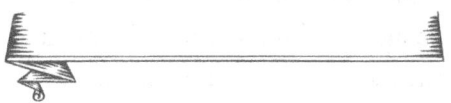

Everyone was waiting for the smoke to clear to see the result of the battle. They all knew better than to celebrate early. They remained vigilant, staring intensely at the center of the smoke.

When it had all cleared, Kalea was still standing somehow. There was no time for them to complain as they had to brace themselves for another round. The only problem was that everyone was at their wit's end.

Rhyen's mark had disappeared and he could barely hold up his bow. Olivia and Vance had to use all their strength so they couldn't cast a single spell. Nathan and Bella had to use their sword and spear, just to support them while they stood.

Regardless, they were ready to give everything they had but Kalea was about to do something that none of them were expecting.

"Well done brave warriors. You have defeated me. I surrender."

None of them was taking her word at face value. So she threw down her weapon and then removed the helm that covered her face. She then proceeded to sit down to tell them about a tale of the past.

When Kalea was seven years old, her little brother appeared in this world. Her parents, being the king and queen of their kingdom, told her that she would have great responsibility for being the future heir to the throne and also a big sister. She was trained to always be an encourager, someone who gave life to others in everything she did.

Because of their parent's busy schedule, Kalea was the primary caretaker of her little brother. She did everything she could to keep him safe and ensure he never took their life for granted. They got along incredibly well as a sister and brother but everything began to change after their parents passed away.

Kalea took her place as the queen in the direst of circumstances. The Mad King's army was growing in power and her kingdom was his next target. His minions lay siege and showed no mercy. The only person spared that day was none other than the queen herself. However, the Mad King doesn't just simply spare one's life. He corrupts them, turning them into his loyal followers.

"But you don't just fight for him. He completely alters the person you once were. I was once known as the queen who encouraged and gave life to others. That's why when I became 'The Fallen' whose powers drain the life force of others."

They all gasped in horror. She allowed the information to sink in and then turned to Bella and Nathan.

"You two fought the Swarm Lord and the Warlock didn't you?" They both nodded.

"The Swarm Lord was once a great king who valued giving power away to everyone regardless of their social standing rather than hoarding it for himself. That's why when he became corrupted, his power allowed him to control the mass of locusts. The Warlock was once a leader who would put his life on the line for his brothers in arms. But because of the Mad King's magic, he became overly obsessed with sacrificing others."

After she finished explaining, Olivia spoke up. "Why are you telling us all this? Aren't you one of the Mad King's loyal subjects?"

"When you become corrupt, you lose your entire mind and become the Mad King's slave. I somehow managed to keep some of my previous memories intact. I had to serve the Mad King with so many of his minions constantly watching my every move. But I always hoped I would be able to find a group of people who would be able to stand up to his tranny. I believe you all have that potential."

As she finished answering Olivia's question, she suddenly started coughing profusely.

"Your wounds are more severe than I anticipated. You have to stop talking now and…" Olivia tried to stop Kalea from speaking further but she continued regardless.

"There isn't much time. You must all protect Queen Victoria from the Mad King. If he captures her, what he did to me, he will surely do the same to her."

"Okay we got it, just stop…" Again she interrupted.

"Also, make sure to keep Bella away from the Mad King. I can't explain it, but she might be your only hope against him."

Many questions began to pile up in their minds but before they could even ask Kalea anything, her right hand was beginning to wither away in the wind.

"It appears my time here is coming to an end."

"No, that isn't going to happen! I'm a cleric, I can use my magic to heal you!" Olivia cast her heal spell but it wasn't working. She tried using stronger iterations of the healing spell but none of it seemed to have any effect.

"Why is nothing working? This shouldn't be happening!" Olivia was still trying but nothing.

"Save your energy young mage. You will need it in your battle against the Mad King." She then looked at everyone else. "I'm sorry for all the trouble I caused. Please stop the Mad King." Then she turned back to Olivia one last time. "And thank you for listening to me and sharing your story..." Those were her last words before her entire body dissipated.

With the former queen gone, everyone looked down in sorrow as another victim was claimed because of the Mad King's reign. They all gain a new resolve to do whatever it takes to bring the Mad King down. There was no time to sulk and little time for discussion as they saw a silver messenger dove flying down towards them.

The dove made its way to Bella and rested on her arm. It had crystal eyes that suddenly began to light up and suddenly, everyone was taken into a different realm where they were met with a woman with a blindfold on. It was none other than Seert.

"Greetings brave warriors. I come to you with an urgent message. By the time you receive this message, the people of Fifthguard will more than likely be fighting against the Mad King's forces. Please make haste, we will hold them off as long as we can."

When Seert finished talking, they all returned to the real world.

"BELLA! Charlotte and everyone back at Fifthguard is in danger!"

"Nathan, stop shouting! I know but how are we going to get back in time? We are so far away from Fifthguard!"

"AHHHHHHH! WHAT ARE WE GOING TO DO, WHAT ARE WE GOING TO DO!"

"Vance, do you think you can do it?" Olivia asked her brother.

"What is he planning to do?" Rhyen asked septically.

"Ummm, I have been practising a spell that allows me to teleport or teleport other things."

"WHAT?! YOU CAN ZIP ZAP TO DIFFERENT PLACES AND YOU DIDN'T TELL US!" Bella then punches Nathan to prevent him from scaring Vance.

"Why didn't you tell us?" Bella asked sincerely.

"Well, ummm, I can only do it sometimes. And when it doesn't work…"

"What happens when it doesn't work?" Rhyen asked.

"Sometimes if it doesn't work, the thing I teleport explodes."

"WHAT? NO EXPLODING NO NO NO!" Nathan yelled.

They were at a loss for what to do as they couldn't come up with any other solution. Even if they could have Vance teleport them without fail, he also specified that the further the distance, the more difficult the spell would be. But with no other option, they were about to take that risk. Until Olivia noticed something secured around Bella's waist.

"Hey, Bella? What's that you got in your belt?"

"Oh, this? It's just some piece of paper that our friend Guranjan gave us." She pulled it out and showed it to everyone.

"You can't be serious. You don't know what this is?!" Rhyen didn't sound impressed.

"She might have told me, but I might not have been listening."

"This is a town portal scroll! It can teleport us to Fifthguard!"

Bella and Nathan looked at each other and in unison, they both had an epiphany, "OHHHH!"

Rhyen just smacked his face, while Olivia was suggesting they used the scroll right away. However, Rhyen warned her that the scroll would only work on one person. It would need an extra boost to have it work for all of them. That was when Olivia and Vance looked at each other and they knew this was their cue.

Olivia took the scroll, opened it up and placed it on a rock. She made sure everyone was standing close together at the perfect distance from the scroll. The most difficult part was getting Nathan to stand still but once they were ready, Olivia and Vance channelled their magical energy towards the scroll, amplifying its power.

The town portal scroll began to glow, activating its power. The ambient blue light surrounded the party and within a few seconds, they all disappeared from the Adenni Plains.

Omen In the Sky

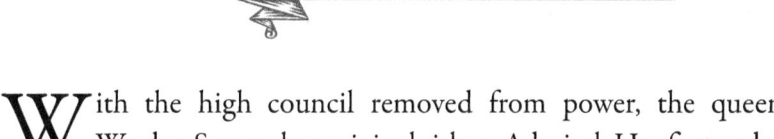

With the high council removed from power, the queen reinstated Warden Sam to her original title as Admiral. Her first order of business was to have all the soldiers ready for battle when the Mad King's army arrived. She had everyone on the training grounds doing push-ups to make sure their endurance and conditioning were up to par.

Also amongst all the soldiers were Rylin, Jett and Rianna. While Rianna was smiling and doing her push-ups, Jett and Rylin did not share the same excitement. The two were complaining about it as Admiral Sam walked by.

"Admiral, I don't see why we have to do these push-ups. I have my shadow beast to call on."

"Jett, you can't rely on that power for everything. Plus you need to be able to control it. These push-ups will help you with that."

He reluctantly sat down and did nothing for the time being. But would eventually do his push-ups. But then there was Rylin to deal with.

"Admiral, I don't see why I have to do these push-ups. I mean, I'm the champion of the Gladiator Games after all!"

Sam had a feeling words would not be enough to convince him. So she decided on a different approach. She called for Rianna, who stopped her push-ups to move towards Sam. The admiral suggested that the two have a quick arm wrestle. Rylin was quite confident in himself while Rianna just simply smiled and agreed.

They placed both their dominant arms on the table as soldiers gathered to watch. Rianna and Rylin each gripped each other's hand and the arm wrestle began.

At the start of the match, Rylin looked to have the advantage as he was pressing down Rianna's arm. But despite the current situation, Rianna still had a smile on her face. Rylin continued to press his advantage and he came inches from winning but things took a turn. Rianna's strength seemed to increase out of nowhere and she powered herself back to where they were back to square one.

Rylin couldn't believe what was happening, but he couldn't lose focus now. He poured all his strength for one final push but it would not be enough. With the same smile, Rianna slowly tired Rylin out and pinned his hand on the table. Rianna was the winner.

After the arm wrestle, all the other soldiers including Rianna and Jett went back to training. But Rylin was still sitting down, wondering how he could have been defeated. When Admiral Sam walked by and saw him sulking, she tried to speak with him.

"Admiral Sam, I don't understand how I lost. I thought I was stronger."

"Rylin, have you considered what Rianna had to go through to become as strong as she is?"

"What do you mean?"

"Your opponent is the youngest of seven. Oh and all her siblings are brothers."

After that conversation, Rylin gained some new perspective and finally understood what Admiral Sam was getting at. From that day on, he vowed to work harder to become stronger and to never be too overconfident about his abilities.

When he got back up, Sam asked Rylin to rejoin everyone who was doing another round of push-ups. Rylin was more than happy to join but when he was about to set foot back into the training ground, a giant shadow loomed over the entire area. Both he and Admiral Sam looked up to see something mysterious blotting out the sky.

In another part of Fifthguard, Zoë, Naaz and Chelsea were down the bazaar area together. Although Chelsea knew exactly where they were going, Naaz didn't and she grew more curious the closer they got.

"Zoë, where in the world are you taking me?"

"Your gauntlets. They are wearing out and you need new ones. I know someone who has the latest items in stock and I can get you them at a special price since I'm the Queen's advisor."

"Hmmm, I don't know. I like the ones I got and it's going to be hard for me to part ways with…"

Before she could finish they were met with Guranjan. She was already notified by Zoë from earlier than she was arriving so she had everything prepared for both Chelsea and Naaz. Chelsea got her upgraded weapons but Naaz saw a shiny new pair of gauntlets with a little bonus that her current ones didn't have.

"OH MY GOSH! THESE HAVE SPIKES ON THE KNUCKLE AREA!" Her eyes were sparkling and she was almost drooling.

"See, I knew you would like them!"

Naaz was about to thank Zoë for her generosity but before she could, a griffin and a dragon came swooping down near them to make an impressive landing. When Leeloo hit the ground, she was immediately greeted by Chelsea with a big hug.

Hopping off the griffin's back were Sebastian, Zaid, and Gia. While Sebastian was excited to announce their arrival, Zaid was trying to get over his flying sickness. And then there was Gia, who wanted to make known to the world about her talents.

"People of Fifthguard! No need to hold your applause. Yes, it is I, Gia, the Glamourous!"

Upon hearing Gia speak, Naaz was not impressed. "Hey, who in the Gladiator Games are you?!"

"Oh was I not clear? I'm GIA THE…"

"That was a rhetorical question! I frankly don't care who you are."

"WHAT?! HOW DARE YOU?! I WILL NOT TAKE THE INSULT OF SOMEONE WHO SOLVES ALL HER SOLUTIONS BY PUNCHING THEM!"

"Then you better get ready because I'm about to solve another problem with these."

Both Gia and Naaz assumed their battle stance, with the witch ready to cast a curse and the brawler armed with her fists. Zoë and Sebastian watched on the sideline, anticipating an epic battle. Leeloo wanted to spectate as well but Chelsea covered her eyes, thinking things would get too vicious. And then there was Zaid who was still feeling sick.

The battle was about to commence but suddenly the sunlight disappeared and a large shadow loomed over them. They all looked up to find that something in the sky was blotting out the sun.

In another area of Fifthguard, Annabelle was waiting inside a laboratory. She was growing impatient so she began to bug Alex.

"Alex hurry up, what is taking so long?"

"Patience! Real science can never be rushed, young citizen!"

"Ugh! How did I get stuck with bodyguard duty all of a sudden? This is way below my pay grade..."

"You aren't getting paid at all! You are doing this for the low, low price of free!"

"Remind me again why I don't just beat you to a pulp?"

"Because you are a kind-hearted individual and would never do something like that!" He said with a nervous smile.

"Sigh, hurry up and finish whatever you are doing already."

"I'm already finished!"

"What? Since when?"

"Oh like five minutes ago."

Annabelle rolled her eyes but she was glad Alex was finally done with his concoction. With that, they were finally able to leave the lab and make their way to meet up with the queen.

"So what were you spending all that time making?"

When Annabelle asked the question, Alex's eyes lit up as he was waiting for this moment the entire time. He pulled the concoction out of his messy hair and then held it out, spotlighting his incredible creation. "TA DA! Feast your eyes on this, the invention that has the potential to bring world peace!"

"Uhh, that just looks like juice of some sort."

"ANNABELLE! HOW DARE YOU! This is the next level in healing potion technology! Also known as HPT!"

"So it heals you a little bit during battle, so what? I hear water works better than potions."

"HAHA! That's where this comes in! This isn't just any ordinary potion! This is known as an ELIXIR! It can heal more than previous potions ever created, it's even more potent than water. Oh and most importantly, it can come in many different flavours..."

Suddenly Annabelle's interest was piqued but their conversation would be cut short as a giant shadow was cast over them. They looked up and what they saw was something blotting out the sky.

Rushing back into the castle were Charlotte, Seert, and Kavan. Having escaped the Mad King's fortress, they made their way to the queen to ensure they received Seert's message.

When they were about to enter the castle grounds, they were immediately halted by a group of palace guards. They were only doing their job, which was protecting the queen but Charlotte was growing impatient. Thankfully, before she lost her cool, the queen happened to appear along with Ava. Victoria told the guards that the three were friends of hers and they lowered their weapons to allow them safe passage.

"Greetings Charlotte, how may I...?"

"Sorry your majesty but there isn't any time for that. The whole realm is in danger and we must..."

"I know, I received your messenger bird and have made preparations to ensure we will be ready when the Mad King arrives."

"No, you don't understand. Seert had another vision, the invasion is going to happen much sooner than expected!"

Victoria turned to face Seert. "You can see visions of the future?"

"Yes, Your Highness. I had a vision that predicted the invasion is coming soon."

"When will the Mad King's army be upon us?"

Before Seert could answer, Kavan felt the need to speak. "Uh guys?"

"Kavan! Now is not the time! Save your announcements for later!" Charlotte yelled.

"But I think you all are going to want to see this."

"What could be so important that it can't..."

As Charlotte was mid-sentence, a shadow was cast over them. Victoria, Seert, and Charlotte looked up in horror at what was blotting out the sky.

"No..." Charlotte said in despair.

"They're here," Seert informed them.

The Artillery

In the sky was a giant portal that had opened above Fifthguard. A fraction of the Mad King's army descended towards the kingdom, bypassing the wall and catching everyone unprepared.

A mixture of goblins and orcs surrounded Annabelle and Alex, preventing them from meeting up with the queen. Then there was a giant Ogre, backed up by a whole battalion of goblins and orcs, that were in the same vicinity as Rianna, Jett, Rylin, and Admiral Sam. Compounding their problems was a once great paladin who had fallen into the Mad King's mind control, who appeared before Naaz, Gia, Zaid, Sebastian, Chelsea, Leeloo, and Zoë. Finally, one of the greatest terrors flew above the sky circling all of Fifthguard, the dread Spectre Rider.

With everyone scattered thin, Seert attempted to send out her messenger birds to communicate with everyone, but there were far too many enemies around that prevented the birds from flying free. They were going to need another way to regroup with everyone. That was when Queen Victoria had an idea.

She told Charlotte that at the top of the castle was a giant war horn that could be heard through the entire kingdom but they needed someone with strong lungs to sound it. Immediately they all looked at Kavan.

"Why is everyone looking at me?"

Charlotte let out a sigh, but she knew it was their only chance. They were about to move towards the location of the war horn but crashing into the castle halls were a band of orcs, riding on the hyenas.

One of the hyenas attempted to take a bite right at Kavan who yelled for help. Thankfully Charlotte kicked the hyena's jaws and caused it to dislocate.

She then had all the hyenas' attention on her and she told Seert to protect the queen and guide Kavan to the war horn.

Charlotte surprised one of the hyena riders by jumping into the air and kicking one of them off their mount. She then pulled the reins of the hyena that she was on and commanded it to run in the opposite direction from Victoria, Ava, Seert, and Kavan. The other hyena riders immediately chased after the lone fighter, leaving the other three free to reach the war horn.

Outside the kingdom walls, a magical blue array of light appeared, indicating where the town portal scroll was about to open. Popping out of it were Bella, Nathan, Rhyen, Olivia and Vance.

"FINALLY! WE ARE OUT OF THE PORTAL AND BACK IN..." Nathan's excitement died down when he realized they were on the outskirts of Fifthguard. The town portal had brought them close but not at the intended spot. They also noticed the ominous portal in the sky.

"It appears the enemy has already begun their assault. We must move quickly or..." Rhyen stopped midway when they heard loud noises coming in the distance. From afar, they could see the Mad King's siege weapons slowly mobilizing toward the entrance of the front gate, ready to bring a frontal assault.

Bella saw that no soldiers were watching the main gate. She realized everyone must have been preoccupied with dealing with the forces being dropped in from the sky portal. The good news was that the ominous portal seemed to be shrinking in size but they still had to deal with the siege weaponry and find a way to get back in the kingdom to reunite the four souls together.

"Ummm, I might have an idea." Vance raised his hand.

"What is it, Vance?" Asked his sister.

"Human Catapult!"

Olivia smacked Vance on the head again. "Vance! We don't need your silly jokes right now! What we need is an actual plan!"

"But I'm serious! Please hear me out!" Vance pleaded and Bella agreed that they should let him continue. "Once those catapults get put into place, we can ambush one of them and use it to launch a few of us back into the city!"

"Hmm, that's not a bad idea but how are we going to do that without any one of us getting flattened?" Rhyen asked inquisitively.

"Olivia's wind magic should be able to help give you a lighter landing."

After hearing Vance explain, they all realized there was a chance the plan could work. The only question they had was who would test the catapult first.

"Hey. Why is everyone looking at me?" Nathan yelled, eventually realizing that he was going to be the guinea pig for the plan.

Meanwhile, the Mad King's ground forces were pushing the siege weapons and mounting them into place. The wheels of the artillery were locked and only the commander and the minions responsible for loading the machinery were on the contraptions. Every other enemy soldier was on the ground, waiting for the siege weapons to strike.

With the ammunition units about to load up the catapults, some arrows flew out of nowhere knocking out one of the commanders and one of the ammunition units. That put all the other minions on high alert but the large group were instantly all knocked up into the air as Nathan came spinning in with his giant sword.

They cleared the path for Bella, Olivia and Vance to advance and take out the remaining group of enemies and secured one of the catapults. Rhyen and Nathan then popped up to the catapult quickly before any reinforcements could disrupt their plans.

Once they were up, both Rhyen and Bella threw Nathan onto the bucket. Once he was on, Olivia cast a wind sphere spell that encased Nathan to protect him from impact. Then they gave the thumbs up for Vance to launch the contraption.

"Uh guys, I changed my mind. Can we think about this first before we... LAUNCHHHHHHHHHHHH!" Nathan shot through the air, knocking down a few of the Mad King's aerial units in the process. He then crashed onto the top walls of the castle but he was relatively unharmed physically.

Seeing their plan work, Rhyen was up next and they repeated the process where he was shielded by the spell and then launched safely onto the castle walls. They had successfully launched everyone they needed to or so Bella thought.

"Bella, you go with those two. Vance and I will find a way to take care of the rest of this machinery."

Bella didn't agree but before she could speak they saw the horde of goblins and orcs racing towards their position. They had caught wind that one of their catapults had been stolen and were ready to claim it back. Bella was ready to fight but Vance snuck up on her and pushed her onto the bucket of the catapult. She tried to get out but Olivia cast the windshield which locked her from moving. Vance then launched her away and she also safely landed on the castle wall.

Olivia and Vance were glad they got everyone over the wall but now they had to turn to their next focus, taking out the artillery. Vance was using a combination of his fire, lightning and ice spells to destroy the first catapult. Olivia saw the oncoming reinforcements heading their way. She used her wind magic to blow the enemy away.

However, their numbers were endless, so Olivia had to switch to casting a barrier spell around the entire catapult. She did her best to hold the forcefield but it was beginning to crack from the minions smashing their weapons against it.

"Hurry it up, Vance! I can't hold this barrier much longer!"

Vance used his ice magic to freeze the critical points of the catapult. Then he struck it with his lightning spell, breaking the support of the entire machinery. Once it was disarmed, Olivia finally lowered the shield allowing the enemy to enter onto the catapult. That was when Vance grabbed his sister by the hand and then used his teleport spell.

The mages vanished, leaving the horde confused but what they also didn't know was the catapult was collapsing. A bunch of them got caught as the parts of the weapon fell onto them, taking out a fair portion of the army.

Reappearing about a kilometre away, Vance and Olivia sat on the ground as they narrowly escaped being surrounded. They high-fived each other to celebrate how they successfully disarmed the catapult but their celebration would be cut short. They looked onward to find that there were many more catapults on their way.

They were already exhausted from taking one down but they refused to quit. They were about to make their way to the next weapon but their path was blocked as the enemy forces reappeared and had them surrounded. Olivia and Vance had no choice, this was where they had to make their stand, but suddenly a squadron of air units came descending towards them. When they set foot onto the ground, they looked at both Vance and Olivia.

These units felt somewhat familiar to Olivia but she couldn't pinpoint why. Their wings were corrupted, their body seemed like it was turned into a special type of metal and they each held a scythe.

"Haha! The reinforcements have arrived! Quick, finish off these two pipsqueaks." Yelled one of the orcs.

Olivia and Vance were ready to take on the insurmountable number of enemies but before they could, the aerial units that had descended upon them made their first move. But in a miraculous turn of events, they didn't attack the twins. Instead, they attacked the Mad King's minions.

Not expecting their treachery, the orcs and goblins were completely caught off guard. Olivia and Vance were shocked by what had happened but one of them turned to Olivia to converse with her.

"You are Olivia aren't you?"

"Yes, but how do you know who I am?"

"Our leader Kalea left us a message as she passed away. She said she had found the hope we had been desperately seeking."

"Oh, I see..." She grew sad, thinking about Kalea again.

"She also told us to assist a healing mage named Olivia on her quest to defeat the Mad King."

"Oh! Why thank you!"

"Our army of the Fallen can take care of these siege weapons for you. I presume you want to regroup with your friends?"

"Yes please!"

She opened her arms to the two mages and carried them as she flew off towards the wall of Fifthguard. As they were flying in the air, they saw the army of the Fallen rebelling against the Mad King's army and taking down the siege weapons.

Attack On Fifthguard

The dark paladin with its flail and shield waited for its challengers to approach. Although there were many warriors within the area to help, Zoë knew they had to separate to contain the damage that was spreading through Fifthguard.

She told Zaid that with his incredible speed, he would be the best option to get all the citizens to safety and away from the crossfire. Zaid wanted to help in combat but he knew he had the best chance to save the most people. With a heavy heart, he agreed to Zoë's idea and he promised that as soon as he was finished, he would return to help them in battle.

After Zaid left, Zoë looked up at the sky and saw the terrifying Spectre Rider that had the castle under surveillance. They had to get rid of that creature so the enemy would lose control of the air. She asked Sebastian if he would be able to send his strongest flying animals to take down the creature.

Sebastian was a bit hesitant as he couldn't think of any animals that would be strong enough to take down the fierce enemy. However, that's when Chelsea looked at Leeloo and she gave her the confident look back.

"Leeloo can take down that creature for you."

"But how? Leeloo is still so tiny, there's no way..."

"Psh! This seems like a job for me! The amazing spectacular and ..."

"OKAY! We get it just do your stupid magic thing already!" Naaz interrupted.

Gia enchanted Leeloo with a spell that caused her to grow in size, strength and tenacity. Chelsea then hopped on Leeloo's back and assured Zoë that they would take down the Spectre Rider. With her new powers, Leeloo flew towards the enemy.

Zoë was going to stay around but Naaz was not too fond of the idea, so she shouted for Sebastian. "Hey, caretaker!"

"Yes, that's me! I'm at your service!"

"Take Zoë to where the queen is."

"OKAY!"

Zoë jumped in. "Wait, I did not agree to this!"

"The people of Fifthguard won't survive without you and the queen's guidance. So don't you dare fight me on this!"

Zoë was shocked by the foresight of Naaz. She didn't expect her to have thought so far ahead. She thanked Naaz for her words and then told her to pummel the paladin to oblivion. To which Naaz said she would gladly do. So Zoë hopped onto the griffin and along with Sebastian, they made their way towards the queen.

Naaz turned around to face her new opponent. She cracked her knuckles as she stood beside Gia.

"Just stay out of my way."

"Please. As if I need your help." Gia responded.

The dark paladin looked on in confusion. "Hmm, it appears there is some disdain amongst you two."

"WE ARE FINE THANK YOU VERY MUCH!" They both responded immediately.

"Good. Because you two won't stand a chance if you are too busy fighting amongst yourselves."

Back in the coliseum, Rianna, Rylin, Jett, and Admiral Sam were met with a giant ogre that had two heads. They shared the same body but they seemed to enjoy arguing with one another.

"Hey Bo, look at the tiny humans down there."

"Quit looking at the silly humans Doof! Let's go crush them!"

The two-headed terror was slowly marching its way towards them. There was plenty of time for the four to come out with a plan to take down the ogre.

"Alright everyone, if we all work together we can take down this creature," Sam suggested and both Rianna and Rylin agreed. Unfortunately, one of them did not.

"Psh, he doesn't look so tough. I can take him myself. Just watch me." Stirring up his temper, he summons his giant shadow beast out to fight. It was clear Jett had much greater control of his powers than before but would it be enough to stop their current foe?

"Hey, Bo look. There's some big shadow thingy. It looks kind of friendly."

"There you go again Doof being you again! That is the enemy, quit getting tricked every time!"

"I'm sorry Bo..."

"No more talking, it's time to ATTACK!"

Jett's shadow pushed everyone else aside and went straight for the ogre. It got the first strike in and looked to have the advantage over the ogre. But after the first punch, the ogre surprised the shadow by casting a multitude of fireballs that burned it.

With Jett's powers weakened, Rylin, Rianna, and Sam tried to intervene and help him but Jett refused. He commanded everyone to stay back and that he would take care of the two-headed ogre himself.

"Hey Bo, that one thinks he can take us all by himself!"

"Well let's show him what a big mistake he's making."

This time the ogre ran towards the shadow beast. The ogre lifted its club midair signalling it was about to cast its fireball spell again. Jett stood still anticipating the attack but Admiral Sam immediately noticed something that no one else knew so she called to Jett.

"Jett, you have to get out of the way!"

"No! I can take this stupid ogre!"

The ogre had its fireball charged and he unleashed it towards the shadow beast but that was not its intended target. The fireball shot straight past the shadow beast leaving Jett confused. He stood still as he finally realized the fireball was aimed at him. He stood still about to take the full force of the attack but thankfully he was pushed out of the crossfire by Admiral Sam.

Jett was unharmed but Sam was severely burned by the attack. When he slowly got back up, he found that his shadow powers had disappeared. Rianna and Rylin rushed to the Admiral's side as she was not moving.

Realizing his mistake, Jett made his way towards Sam and found her unconscious but still breathing. He looked to both Rianna and Rylin, hoping they could forgive him for his foolish actions. They forgave him and agreed to work together to take down the two-headed ogre.

The two-headed ogre had left, assuming it had won when Jett's shadow disappeared. It was about to cause terror on the innocent civilians but one of them felt a rock hit his head.

"Hey, you big dummy! Why don't you pick on someone your own size?" Rylin yelled.

Rylin got one of the ogre's attention and it turned around and swung its club at the small warrior. Because of its bulky size, the swing was so slow, that Rylin had more than enough time to run away and hide.

"Doof! What are you doing wasting our time with that little runt!"

"But Bo! He called me a big dummy! He hurt my feelings!"

"Doof you are a dummy! You fell for his taunt! Just ignore him and let..."

As the smarter head was trying to refocus, Rianna snuck through the rooftops and jumped onto the shoulder of the ogre. With the ogre still confused, Rianna shouted as loud as she could, destroying the eardrums of the smarter ogre.

Rianna remained on the shoulder of the ogre forcing it to try to slap her off, but Rianna was too quick and he slapped his counterpart's face instead.

"Doof! What are you doing!"

"I'm sorry Bo! I don't know what to do! Please tell me!"

"I can't hear anything!"

While they were still confused, Rylin had a rope in his hands and he began to wrap it around one of the ankles of the giant. Doof shifted his focus onto Rylin as he saw him beneath its foot but then Rianna shouted from across the rooftop to distract him again. He slammed the rooftops but missed the peppy squire.

Bo saw Doof unable to follow what the enemy was doing so he yelled to get his attention. Doof finally listened and then he turned to see Jett who was standing alone not too far away. Doof grew overconfident because he had easily defeated Jett before, so how would this time be any different?

Jett summoned his shadow beast and it charged straight at the two-headed giant. Doof and Bo were both ready for the shadow's assault. As they raised their club, they readied themselves to cast a fireball but they felt something pulling one of their legs. It was Rylin who had tied the rope and was now pulling it to distract them.

Doof was again distracted but Bo told him to stay focused on Jett. So Doof managed to ignore Rylin for a bit but then Rianna reappeared on his shoulder and began punching him on the side of the head. Doof was too confused and right when Jett's shadow was in range to strike, Rianna jumped out of the way and the two-head ogre had no way to defend itself.

Jett's shadow creature struck both the heads of the ogre and it fell on its back against the ground in defeat. With its fading consciousness, they both wondered how they could have lost to some puny humans. What the ogre failed to realize was that they didn't lose because of one person. They lost because Rylin, Rianna and Jett were able to work together and execute the strategy needed to beat the ogre. A strategy that Admiral Sam devised.

After seeing the two head ogre close its eyes, the three warriors were finally able to take a rest. They helped each other back up as they heard a loud sound coming from the Queen's castle. The war horn had sounded.

Battle for the Sky

Surveilling the kingdom from the sky was the Spectre Rider on its flying serpent. It had complete sight of what was happening through Fifthguard and was ready to direct the Mad King's army with its knowledge. It had free reign of the skies until Chelsea and Leeloo showed up ready for a showdown but her enemy didn't seem very impressed.

"Diamondlot must be desperate to send a teenager and a baby dragon in disguise to fight me."

Leeloo lost her temper and wanted to bite him but Chelsea knew better and kept her restrained. "Ha, don't go crying home when you lose to us then."

"Insolent girl! I'll show you the meaning of true despair!"

The Spectre Rider unleashed its aura which blew them back but Leeloo managed to regain her composure and keep them afloat. They wouldn't have much time to rest as the flying serpent rushed in to attack Leeloo. While the two creatures were scraping against each other, the rider pulled out its sword hoping to catch Chelsea off guard but she drew her sword to block the attack.

The four continued to struggle, not giving the other an inch. They were locked in a stalemate until the serpent spat into Leeloo's eyes. The rider then knocked Chelsea off her dragon and she began falling from the sky. Leeloo wanted to help but she was occupied by the enemy.

Chelsea was beginning to drop but before she could accelerate further, she fell on something soft. Despite feeling a bit of pain she opened her eyes to see a couple of familiar faces: Zoë and Sebastian.

"Howdy partner!" Sebastian said with excitement.

"What...? How come you are both here?" Chelsea asked in confusion.

"We thought you could use a bit of help. Couldn't let you and Leeloo face that monstrosity by yourselves."

Chelsea was grateful they had turned around but now they had to focus on finding a way to defeat the Spectre Rider. But first, they had to save Leeloo.

Leeloo did her best to defend herself as the Spectre Rider continued its brutal assault. The serpent kept whipping her with its tail and with her vision temporarily impaired, Leeloo slammed against the ground. Being as persistent as she was, she continued to stand up on her own but the Spectre cast a spell to keep her immobilized. Now the serpent was ready to bite against her neck and inject its venom into her.

As the serpent pounced towards Leeloo, a lasso appeared and wrapped around its mouth, forcing it to close. Chelsea now had control of the serpent's mouth and she pulled hard on the rope and caused the serpent to react violently. The creature was now swinging out of control and giving its rider some problems.

With the Spectre Rider preoccupied, Sebastian and his griffin swung in and tackled them. The griffin followed up and slammed into their opponent several more times. But eventually, the Spectre Rider regained control of the situation. The serpent managed to take a bite on the griffin's neck and then the rider knocked Sebastian off his companion.

The griffin was now poisoned and barely able to breathe. Sebastian, who was lying on the ground, saw his companion in pain and attempted to reach out to help but the Spectre Rider returned and stood between them. With its sword in its hand, it was ready to eliminate the animal caretaker. The rider lifted its blade but it was blindsided as Leeloo and Chelsea tackled them aside.

"You two again!"

"Aww did you miss us?"

The serpent attempted to use its spit attack again but Leeloo was prepared this time and countered by unleashing fire from her mouth. With the attack neutralized, both riders commanded their companion to tackle each other at full speed. The impact was so great that both riders were knocked off their mounts.

Leeloo and the flying serpent continue their battle by taking to the sky again, but this time without their riders. The serpent wasted no time as it used its body and coiled around her enemy. Leeloo struggled to break free so instead of staying in the air, she dove straight for the ground.

The serpent refused to let go so the two stubborn creatures continued to dive straight into the ground until they hit on impact. The collision allowed Leeloo to break free but she sustained some damage. Both creatures got up and began bashing their heads against one another, and it seemed they were locked into a stalemate until the serpent used its tail lash attack against Leeloo's face.

Leeloo's head hit the side of a building and she was knocked down onto the ground where she was unconscious. She was defenseless with the serpent ready to inject its venom into her body. The serpent opened its fangs and lunged forward.

Midway into its attack, Leeloo's eyes suddenly opened and she used her fire breathing when the serpent was in point-blank range. The serpent took a mouthful of flames and its lungs were suffering from the burning effects of Leeloo's fire. Leeloo then grabbed a hold of the serpent and pinned it to the ground where she used her fire to incinerate her opponent. She had claimed victory as the superior apex creature.

Not far away, Chelsea continued to battle against the Spectre Rider who had lost his pet. The rider swung his blade which Chelsea partially blocked but his power was so overwhelming, the wind caused scratches on her face.

"Surrender foolish human. You are no match for me."

Despite the cuts on her face, Chelsea refused to give in. The rider was infuriated by her tenacity and so he swung his blade again.

Chelsea rolled out of danger to create some distance between her and her enemy. She pulled out her lasso and tangled it around her opponent's sword. The rider thought she was going to pull his weapon away but instead, Chelsea rushed in and kicked the Spectre.

As the Spectre was pushed back, Chelsea pulled on the lasso and stole the weapon from the rider. She tossed the weapon away and charged in with her sword and drove it into his gut. Chelsea landed the critical blow and the Spectre was frozen and unable to move.

Seeing her enemy defeated, Chelsea attempted to retrieve her weapon, but her sword was stuck. Then the Spectre's hand suddenly grabbed Chelsea's arm and it began to burn in pain. Chelsea managed to pull her arm away but the Spectre kicked her against the ground.

Even though Chelsea was able to get up, her dominant hand was in severe pain without any strength. The Spectre slowly approached her, pulling out the sword she drove into him.

"You have my respect for surviving this long, but I have defeated many great warriors and kings before you were even a child. I will give you an honourable…"

He couldn't finish his sentence because a sword was suddenly driven through his chest. The Spectre was yelling in pain and as it turned around to look, it saw the one responsible for his demise, Zoë.

"Human… How…?"

"The shopkeeper Guranjan gave me this sword earlier. It's infused with magic specifically designed to deal with enemies like you."

"Argh!" It reached out its hand to try and grab Zoë but when his hand came within inches of making contact, his whole body disintegrated and its ashes were blown into the wind.

Zoë reached out her hand to pull Chelsea up and as they stood side by side, they saw Leeloo flying in with Sebastian on her back. They made a soft landing and the warriors stood together, looking upon their shared victory against the dreaded Spectre Rider. The skies of Fifthguard were free once again as they heard the sound of the warhorn.

Battle Against the Paladin

The dark paladin stood tall while Naaz and Gia were both heavily breathing. It was clear they attempted to take on the paladin individually without either one having much success. Having had a relatively easy time dealing with them so far, he decided to make things a bit more interesting.

"It is a shame."

"What are you babbling about?" Naaz asked.

"By yourself, you both are very skilled in your arts, but neither of you stand a chance fighting me alone."

Naaz was furious with what her opponent said. She rushed into him and threw her barrage of punches but her spiked gauntlets were met with the paladin's shield.

"Imprudent girl, you tried this before."

"I don't care! Your shield will have to break eventually! I'll keep smashing it until I get through!"

So Naaz kept throwing her punches but what she didn't realize was that every time she hit his shield, it was storing energy. The paladin was waiting to reflect all the energy at once at Naaz to finish her in one attack but Gia caught wind of his strategy.

She tried to warn Naaz but she was too focused to listen. The paladin stood waiting for Naaz to land one final punch before he unleashed his counterattack. Thankfully Gia interrupted Naaz's attack by striking the shield first with a ranged spell. She set off the paladin's counter ability early so Naaz only received a minor hit from the implosion. However, she was not happy with Gia's interference.

"What do you think you are doing?!"

"What do I think I'm doing?! I just saved your life!"

"I don't need your help! I got this situation all under control."

As Naaz turned her back to Gia, the witch cast a spell on her, turning the brawler into a greck. She tried yelling insults at the caster but all her words were gibberish and she lost the ability to speak.

"Oh sorry dear, I can't quite understand you. Just sit and watch as I, the great Gia, take care of this novice paladin!"

The paladin was not in a speaking mood, he swung his flail at Gia who propelled herself back to stay out of melee range. Knowing physical attacks would be useless, she controlled the rocks and rubble around her and used her magic to direct them at her enemy. The paladin was able to use his shield to block the incoming projectiles but he couldn't use his counter move.

"For a loudmouth witch, you are quite smart."

"Ha, I got more tricks up my sleeve."

"And so do I."

The paladin surprised Gia by throwing his shield at her. She barely dodged it as it cut off a bit of her hair. She thought she was now safe but then she heard the shield ricochet off the wall and then separate into three smaller shields and they were all boomeranging back to her.

She cast a spell to protect herself from the incoming shields but they continued to bounce off the walls and then back against her forcefield. The barrier was beginning to crack and it was clear it wouldn't hold up for long, and the paladin knew it.

Forced into a corner, Gia knew playing defense forever was no longer an option. So when the shield bounced off her forcefield again, she let go of her defense and then fired a curse directly at the paladin. Without his shield, he was unable to defend himself but the curse seemed to have absolutely no effect on the paladin.

Gia looked on in disbelief as her curse had no immediate effect. At the same time, the shields came back and all struck her at the same time. Gia was now down on her knees and the paladin stood in front of her with only his flail in hand.

"You have been a worthy adversary, but unfortunately, you are still just a foul witch at the end of the day. You must be brought to justice." Channelling his powers, his flail suddenly turned into a giant hammer that was pulsing with dark energy.

Gia looked at the mighty weapon and then closed her eyes knowing this could be her demise. The paladin raised the giant hammer and shouted, "Begone foul being!" But the hammer was never dropped against Gia. Instead, Naaz appeared and delivered a combination of punches right at the paladin's plate mail.

Naaz then finished off her consecutive strikes with a roundhouse kick to push the paladin back. She had successfully fended off the paladin who was confused as to how she was able to sneak up on him, but then it came to him.

"You... you transformed her into that monstrosity on purpose! So that I wouldn't detect her presence." he directed his comment at Gia who was smiling.

"Haha, pretty clever huh?"

"So all this time, you were pretending to hate each other to get me to let my guard down."

"Oh no, we do hate each other. It disgusts me that I needed her help." Naaz commented.

"You're welcome!" Gia shouted to Naaz as they continued their banter.

"ENOUGH! Both your arrogance has gone too far. I will cleanse this world from the two of you!"

"Oh, don't worry about it, this battle is already over," Gia said with confidence.

The paladin was confused until he noticed that his armour was suddenly cracking and he began to feel pain from within. "What? What did you do to me?" Then he remembered the curse that Gia placed on him earlier that seemed to have no effect.

"You tricked me again! You knew that curse wouldn't have any immediate effect!"

Gia stuck her tongue out. It was a curse that weakened the paladin's armour, allowing Naaz to easily break it down with her punch. In addition, the curse also amplified all the damage the paladin would receive.

"I WILL NOT LOSE TO A MINDLESS BRUTE AND A CURSED WITCH!"

He had completely lost his composure and unleashed all the power he had left. On the other hand, Naaz calmly appeared in front of him and landed one more punch where the curse was cast. That was the final strike needed to cause the paladin an immense amount of pain and have all his power backfire on him.

Gia was still on her knees but she saw Naaz extend an open hand. She was hesitant at first but she gladly accepted the help.

"We tell no one what just happened," Naaz demanded.

"My thoughts exactly." Gia agreed.

Once they were both standing, they heard the sound of the war horn in the distance. They made their way towards the sound.

King's Arrival

Alex and Annabelle were making their way to where they heard the sound of the warhorn but a brigade of goblins and orcs blocked their path. Annabelle had no problem dealing with her enemies as she was far superior in skill. Unfortunately, their numbers seemed endless and from afar she heard someone's voice.

"Annabelle! They are abducting me again! HELP!" Alex yelled.

"Sigh! Why is it always me?" She was annoyed but she easily sliced through all her enemies and then grabbed Alex by the collar. Then she threw him over her shoulder and began running away from the minions.

"Annabelle! Stop, the blood is all rushing to my brain and..." She had enough of his bickering so she put a piece of tape and covered his mouth.

"There! Much better." And she continued on her way.

Back at the castle, Seert, Victoria, Ava and Kavan were making their way towards the war horn. They were now on the highest floor of the castle where it was exposed to the sky. When they looked down, they saw Charlotte on the hyena staring down four other hyena riders.

One of them threw a rope hoping to pull her away from her mount. But instead, Charlotte grabbed hold of the rope and commanded her hyena to circle the other four riders. One of the orcs was smart enough to tell its mount to get out of the way but the other three just stayed and starred.

Eventually, the rope fully wrapped around three of the orcs and with one big pull from Charlotte, she took out three of her enemies in one move. That left the one orc rider who pulled out his scimitar, ready to charge at Charlotte.

They converged against one another, the orc with its blade and Charlotte who seemed unarmed. As the hyenas met, the orc swung the scimitar to strike Charlotte, but she jumped into the air to avoid the attack. Charlotte then landed on the enemy's hyena and kicked the orc off his mount. The hyenas seeing their riders all defeated, scurried away in fear.

Ava, Kavan, Seert, and Victoria saw all that had happened and were in awe at how Charlotte easily defeated her enemies. It had them thinking that no one stood a chance against Charlotte. But someone made an unexpected arrival that caused everyone to shiver in fear.

Standing on the opposite side of the battlefield from Charlotte, the Mad King gave an unsettling smile. Victoria knew Charlotte needed help so everyone immediately turned around to reach the warhorn. Unfortunately, a squadron of giant flying beetles landed with more of the Mad King's minions aboard.

Knowing the priority was to get Kavan to the warhorn, Seert cast her illusion magic to distract the enemy. She told everyone to move on ahead while she held the illusion up. Victoria, Kavan and Ava thanked her for her efforts and continued without their comrade.

When the three drew closer to the warhorn, another squadron of beetles appeared, except these appeared by crawling over the walls of the castle. One of them spooked Kavan, leaving him paralyzed in fear. Thankfully, Victoria pulled out her scepter and smacked the beetle off the wall and it tumbled down the castle. Both Kavan and Ava were surprised to see this side of Victoria.

"What are you two doing? GO!" She shouted to the two of them.

Kavan and Ava snapped out of their admiration and continued to advance. Victoria then turned around to face the oncoming swarm that was climbing up the walls. She faced them alone but she was much tougher than any of the enemies anticipated. One by one she smacked the beetles aside to stall time for Kavan.

Ava and Kavan could see the war horn in sight and they were very close to reaching it. But once again, their way was blocked as two more orcs riding on their beetles appeared. Kavan looked for options to get around them but there were none.

"Oh no! AVA! What are we going to do?!" He put his hands on her shoulder and shook her but Ava didn't say anything and just smiled back. "AVA! Talk!"

The two beetles charged towards them at full speed. Kavan closed his eyes anticipating the worst but when nothing happened for an extended period, he reopened his eyes. He looked around to find the beetles and the orcs lying on their backs defeated. He was confused as to what happened and he turned to the only other person who was with him.

"Uhh, Ava. Did you...?" Again Ava just smiled and then she gave a quick reply. "Don't you have something to do?" Kavan remembered about the war horn, so he quickly rushed towards it, but he would never look at Ava the same again.

The Mad King had finally arrived. Charlotte knew that this day was inevitable but she wasn't expecting it to be this soon. The king stood in his jester-like outfit, applauding Charlotte.

"Well done Charlotte. Out of all the humans I have captured, you have been the greatest surprise."

"Save your breath. Flattery will get you nowhere."

"So serious! Even after all I've done for you."

Charlotte had heard enough. She reacted by throwing a dagger she had hidden in her sleeves to try and catch the Mad King off guard. He easily dodged the attack but Charlotte immediately followed up by attempting to strike him down with multiple jabs. But the Mad King was no stranger to combat. He continued to avoid all of Charlotte's attacks with ease and it was obvious she was growing tired and frustrated.

Finally, the Mad King was done playing games. He stopped one of Charlotte's kicks by grabbing her leg then flung her around and threw her against the ground. Charlotte, refusing to give up, attempted to bounce back but the Mad King cast a dark binding spell that had her chained and unable to move.

"So predictable as always. I already knew your plan before you escaped. How you wanted to assemble a team to locate the four souls of the legendary warrior."

"You knew everything?!"

"Everything!" His reply had Charlotte looking down in defeat.

"Funny. You did all that work to find others who could help you fight against me. But in the end, you are all alone and no one is coming to help you!"

He held out his hand ready to cast one final spell but before he could end it, he heard a sound coming in the distance that couldn't be ignored. It was the sound of the war horn, which meant Kavan and the others were successful in their quest. That thought alone gave Charlotte hope.

"Ha, no matter. It's too late. I will lay waste to this entire resistance of yours, starting with you." The Mad King directed his focus on Charlotte but again he felt danger approaching from behind, so he cast a shield that blocked a volley of arrows that came his way.

Then spinning at incredible speed with his giant sword, Nathan slammed his weapon which just missed the Mad King. His goal was to force the Mad King away from Charlotte. Bella then appeared in front of Charlotte to ensure she was safe. Reinforcements had arrived.

The Four United

The atmosphere was tense as the Mad King stood on the other side facing his enemies. He had to worry about Nathan from the front line and he spotted Rhyen attacking him from afar. And then there was the anomaly of Bella, whose presence he couldn't detect. Despite how serious the environment was, Bella took a moment to turn around to see if Charlotte was okay.

"CHARLOTTE!" Bella gives her a big hug, making her feel slightly awkward.

"Uhhh, yeah. I missed you too, I guess?"

Charlotte was trying to get Bella to let go but she held on tight. While that was happening, the Mad King continued to study Bella. He was perplexed as to why he couldn't sense her at all when he could easily detect everyone else's aura.

As he was pondering about Bella's presence, Rhyen and Nathan thought they could take advantage of his position. Rhyen gave Nathan some cover fire by launching some arrows towards the king. Unfortunately, the Mad King saw right through their attacks. Nathan's sneak attack didn't work as the Mad King grabbed him in midair. He then held him in front, using him as a shield, forcing Rhyen to cease fire. In his hesitation, The Mad King grabbed Nathan's giant sword and threw it at Rhyen. He managed to avoid taking the full hit from the weapon but the impact sent him hitting his back against the castle wall.

With Rhyen out of the picture, the Mad King was about to use his dark magic against Nathan. However, Bella refused to let that happen as she charged in with her spear to interfere.

Again the Mad King was caught by surprise as he couldn't sense her attack, forcing him to drop Nathan. Bella was the only one who was currently able to fight against the Mad King. Despite the odds, she was ready to take him on all by herself but the Mad King held out his hand, applauding her.

"Well well, what an interesting turn of events. I was very confused at first but now I understand what's going on here."

"What are you on about you crazy king?"

"Oh, you won't even believe me if I told you!"

Charlotte tried to tell Bella not to listen to the Mad King as he tried to get into her head. But her interest had been piqued and she had to know. She fought the Mad King demanding him to tell her and slowly he told her everything. No one else could hear them but throughout the fight, Bella was becoming more distracted.

Eventually, he disappeared and then reappeared behind Bella. He then placed one of his hands on her shoulder and cast a spell that caused her to faint on the ground.

Seeing his friend lying unconscious, Nathan picked up his sword and charged recklessly at the Mad King. Charlotte saw Nathan yelling into battle and knew she couldn't let him fight alone so she forced herself up and attacked the Mad King as well.

In unison, both Charlotte and Nathan attempted to strike the Mad King together but his magic held them in midair. He then sent them both slamming against the walls. With both of them wounded from the attack, the Mad King slowly made his way towards Nathan.

He was ready to pick Nathan up by his throat but before his hand could reach, Zaid dashed in and pulled Nathan to safety. He then returned to the battlefield ready to fight the Mad King and he wasn't alone. Standing behind him were the other three warriors who shared the legendary warrior's soul: Annabelle, Naaz, and Rhyen stood ready to fight him.

The Mad King saw the four warriors with all their marks glowing, indicating that they were using their full power. Before the king could make a move, Zaid ran circles around him. While he was trying to lock in on Zaid's location, Naaz appeared in front of the Mad King and performed her combo strike.

Naaz's punches came fast and furious, but the Mad King maintained his footing and blocked all of her attacks. She then jumped away from him because Rhyen launched a volley of arrows in his direction. But instead of the arrows flying directed at the Mad King, they got swallowed into the tornado that Zaid created from his incredible speed.

When enough arrows were fired into the tornado, Zaid controlled when to release the arrows at his opponent. They came from many different directions, giving the Mad King a difficult time to sense where the attacks were coming from. He deflected many but some got to him, giving him minor wounds.

With his speed slightly hindered, Naaz jumped back into the fight and threw the strongest punch she had. She landed her fist right on the Mad King's jaw and his body dragged against the ground from the impact.

When he regained some of his composure after the attack, he slowly got up but he didn't notice Annabelle was now behind him. In one second, Annabelle's katana pierced through the Mad King's heart. He fell to his knees and his eyes slowly shut.

Knowing not to let their guard down, the four warriors remained vigilant as this could have been one of his tricks. Annabelle was about to pull out her sword from the Mad King while Naaz, Zaid, and Rhyen slowly approached him.

At this time, Charlotte picked herself up from the ground and saw the four warriors getting closer to the Mad King. She knew it was a trap and shouted for them to run away. They heard her voice but it was too late.

Suddenly the Mad King's eyes were open and he immediately grabbed Annabelle's right hand and her hand began to burn. At the same time, he released a dark pulse from his hand that struck both of Zaid's legs, rendering him unable to run.

Naaz was furious with what the Mad King had done so in her rage, she attempted to land another punch but he easily dodged the attack and grabbed her arm. Rhyen had his arrow aimed and ready to fire but he couldn't as the Mad King held Naaz in front as a hostage.

Rhyen held his shot back so the Mad King threw both Naaz and Annabelle at him, knocking them all together. With all four warriors in close proximity, he cast a spell that had them bound in shackles and unable to fight back. He walked up to them and held out his hand.

"I will be taking these back now." As he spoke, the marks on the four warriors were being siphoned away and they reappeared on the Mad King's body instead. Charlotte looked in horror as she couldn't comprehend what had happened, so the Mad King revealed his malicious scheme.

"How? How are you able to steal the legendary warrior's soul?"

"Ha! So easily fooled as always. I had my agents spread lies about the legendary warrior's soul being split into four. His soul was never shattered to pieces but something else was."

That was when Charlotte realized what the four marks represented. "No, it can't be..."

"Yes!" He held out his hand and appearing before Charlotte's eyes was the Mad King's lost weapon, Desolator.

Lost Soul

Charlotte looked at the grim situation she was in. The Mad King had reclaimed his ultimate weapon and the four warriors that were supposed to defeat him were powerless to stop him. Despite how awful the situation looked, she still got up and refused to give in.

The Mad King laughed at her feeble attempt to stop him. He thought she was going to face him all by herself but she was not alone. Appearing to help her were other fighters ready to stand up to his tranny.

The twin mages Olivia and Vance struck their pose. Gia made her grand entrance. Sebastian crashed in, riding on his bullboar. Zoë rode into battle with her stallion. Leeloo flew in with Chelsea on her back. Rylin let out a warcry into the fight. Alex came in with his messy hair. Guranjan walked in with a bag full of mysterious goods. Kavan carried a warhorn, ready to sound off. Jett called on his shadow beast, stomping in. Ava quietly waltzs into the arena. Rianna stormed in with her lance and her peppy attitude. And then there was Seert and Victoria who stood by Charlotte to make sure she was okay.

The Mad King stood alone with his sword without a drop of sweat down his face. He told them all to attack him at once. Everyone except Seert, Victoria and Charlotte engaged against the Mad King.

"So you got another plan right?" the queen asked.

"No. I'm afraid I'm out of ideas." Responded Charlotte.

The two looked down in defeat but Seert had some words of hope. "Wait, we might still have a chance."

Charlotte and Victoria's spirits lifted as they asked Seert for more details. She pointed to Bella who was still unconscious and told them that she saw a vision of her squaring off against the Mad King. Victoria asked to find out what happened at the end of her vision but Seert never saw the victor.

That was when Charlotte remembered Bella's early bout with the Mad King. Although it didn't end too favourably, the Mad King had trouble detecting her presence. Charlotte now had a plan, they were going to stall as long as they could, hoping Bella would regain her consciousness.

Although Bella was unconscious, she was awake within her mind. She was initially confused as to where she was but after recalling her tilt against the Mad King, she figured out where she was. Then she began thinking about what the Mad King said to her before she fainted.

The Mad King revealed to Bella that she was no longer alive. She didn't believe him at first but she couldn't shake out of her mind what he said. When asked about her past, Bella couldn't recall anything past the time she found herself on the boat heading to Fifthguard. Bella denied it by saying she had amnesia but the Mad King said that the reason she lost her memory was because she had lost her life.

Her mind was beginning to go insane from all the thoughts poisoning her mind. She would have lost her sanity but someone appeared to her whose presence was calming.

"It's you again. The mean person who woke me up last time!"

"I guess I did that. But I hope you know, that being mean to you is not the only reason I'm here."

"So why are you here then?"

"To help you figure out the truth from the lies. And to help you accept what you can change and that which you cannot."

"Easy for you to say, Mr. Legendary Warrior."

"So the Mad King had already told you?"

"Sort of. I guess I always sort of had a feeling." She reminisced about times when she survived the unthinkable: In her battle against Jett's Shadow Beast, surviving being bitten by countless ravenous locusts, when she couldn't be offered as a live sacrifice to the leviathan, and when she survived Kalea's attack.

The man took a moment to allow Bella to take in what she said before speaking again. He explained to her what happened in his battle against the

Mad King. As they separated Desolator from the Mad King, the legendary warrior's soul was about to be lost.

"One of the wizards used their magic to transfer my soul into another body. Unfortunately, his spell failed at the time and my soul was left wandering for many years.

Until one day I found a village that was under siege by the Mad King's army. I saw a woman who was protecting her daughter who had suffered major injuries. She came to the water with nowhere else to run and the enemy pursuing her. With her last efforts, she placed her daughter onto a small boat and kicked it out to sea."

"That girl... it's me isn't it?"

"Yes, your condition that day was near fatal. You were in the middle of the sea with no land in sight. There was no telling how much longer you could have held on for as over time, your soul was beginning to fade away."

"So it is true. I'm only here because of your soul. I don't exist... Everything I have done is meaningless."

Her mind was still clouded by the Mad King's spell so the man took matters into his own hands. He pulled a bamboo stick and smacked her in the head.

"OW! What was that for?!"

"You'll be fine, you have a thick skull. Besides, this is all in your imagination anyway so it's not like I actually hit you on the head."

Although it was true, Bella still felt the pain at the moment. But at the same time, she was thankful as her head felt clearer.

"Tell me, Bella, do you think all you have done has been meaningless?"

Bella was still recovering from the hit, so she asked him to elaborate.

"Think about everyone you have met through your journey. All these brave characters were scattered throughout the realm and how they would have never met each other. You have made an impact on every single one of these people and look at what they are doing now?"

Suddenly, the man showed her a glimpse of what was happening back in the real world. Bella could see everyone putting aside all their differences to stand against the Mad King. "Everyone, they are fighting together."

"Correct. Very few could have united all these people for a common cause."

Bella continued watching and she noticed Charlotte telling everyone to hold on as they were stalling for her return. At that moment, the Mad King's spell was completely lifted and Bella's mind was freed. She then turned to the man who had helped her.

"Still think your life is meaningless?"

For once Bella was left without anything to say but she heard a voice calling out. "BELLA! BELLA! WAKE UP! WE NEED YOU!" It sounded like Kavan.

The man smiled, "Well you better get on your way. Your friends have struggled long enough."

Before he left, Bella managed to get a few words out of her mouth, "Thank you, legendary warrior!"

"Psh, the name is Rice."

And they both disappeared from her mind.

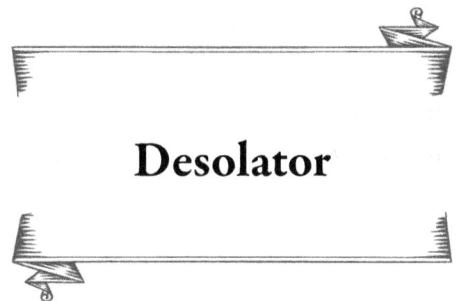

Desolator

The Mad King stood alone as he faced off against what was left of the resistance. He had no fear as he possessed 'Desolator' once again and he was about to show them its true power.

Olivia, Vance, and Gia made the first moves as they cast their strongest magic in unison. The three combined to form a magical tri-attack that was heading straight for the Mad King. He held up his weapon, which was in the shape of a sword but it magically changed into a giant shield.

The Mad King placed the shield in front of himself and the tri-attack bounced off with each of the spells sent back against their casters. The witch and the two mages were taken out by their attacks and the other warriors were left wondering how the Mad King's weapon transformed.

He revealed to the rest of them that 'Desolator' was the true weapon of chaos. It was a weapon that had a mind of its own, transforming into whatever it wanted without any regard for the wielder's preference or need.

Upon hearing about Desolator's true power, Ava pulled out a lasso from Guranjan's equipment bag and threw it at the Mad King's arm. It wrapped around the Mad King's wrist and with a powerful pull from Ava, she forced the Mad King to drop his weapon.

He was annoyed by Ava and ready to strike her down but Rianna and Rylin came rushing in with their lance and Morningstar to disrupt his focus. The two warriors thought their opponent was unarmed but they were deceived. The Mad King reached out with his left hand and his shield returned to his hand in an instant. Rianna and Rylin saw the weapon had returned to their enemy but they continued to press the attack.

Desolator changed again, turning itself into a chain weapon. The Mad King first surprised Ava by suddenly pulling on the rope tangled around his right wrist with all his might. Now Ava was pulled towards Rianna and Rylin, knocking them both from behind. He then whirled his chain weapon wildly against the three fighters and overpowered them completely.

The Mad King had taken out six fighters in a relatively short time but out of nowhere, he was bumped into and sent against the castle wall by Sebastian's bullboar. "Atta boy, Coco! Let's hit him again!" So again, they charged at their enemy but this time he was ready.

With his weapon changing into a whip, he lashed at Coco by hitting her right in the forehead. That disrupted Coco's focus and Sebastian lost control of her. The Mad King used the whip again, this time making Coco blind with anger and she ran head-first against a wall. Sebastian managed to safely jump off Coco and he wanted to check on his pet to see if she was okay. But the Mad King used the whip to restrain him and slam him to the ground.

Kavan and Alex were looking to join in but both Victoria and Zoë intervened. Zoë asked Alex to check in on Zaid, Naaz, Rhyen and Annabelle to see if he could do anything to improve their condition. Then Victoria turned and requested for Kavan to do all he could to wake Bella up. They both went to do what they were asked and the two women turned around to face their dreaded foe.

"Both the queen and her trusted advisor. It must be my lucky day."

Zoë wasted no time as she commanded her stallion to dash towards her enemy. Again, Desolator transformed, this time into a giant maul that he held in one hand. Zoë's steed leaped into the air and was ready to strike the Mad King but he slammed the head of the maul onto the ground creating a massive shockwave that sent both Zoë and her stallion against the walls.

The Mad King appeared in front of Zoë as she attempted to get up. He was ready to drop the hammer down. However, the queen intercepts the attack by parrying the maul against her scepter. Victoria was doing her best to protect Zoë but it was clear she would eventually be overwhelmed by the Mad King's strength.

Thankfully, Leeloo swiped the Mad King out of the way with her giant claws and protected the queen. Chelsea then told Leeloo to take to the skies and then unleash her fire-breathing attack on the Mad King. Quick to react, he whirled the maul in his hand to create a windshield that deflected the flames away from him.

Leeloo and Chelsea remained high in the sky thinking there was no way the Mad King could reach them but they were wrong. Desolator shifted into a deadly boomerang, which the Mad King threw at his target in the sky. Leeloo dodged the initial attack and Chelsea was perspective enough to know that the attack would return but they weren't ready for what happened next.

Not only did the boomerang curve around from behind but it split into five separate shards. Leeloo evaded two of them but one of them hit Chelsea and knocked her off her companion. Now Chelsea was falling and Leeloo attempted to dive down to grab her but two more of the boomerang shards hit against her wings and exploded on impact.

After the explosion, Leeloo reverted to normal size as Gia's magic had worn off. She too was dropping at a dangerous speed and to make matters worse, she was unconscious.

Chelsea saw the predicament they were in and she looked around to find what options she had left. She reached around her waist and found her trusty lasso. Despite being in midair and falling, she managed to throw the rope and wrap it around Leeloo, pulling them together. She wrapped her arms around the dragon, and she made sure she would be the first to hit the ground, taking most of the impact.

She closed her eyes waiting for her body to hit the ground but Seert would not allow it to happen. She summoned a flock of her birds and commanded them to lighten their fall. The birds all went below Chelsea and began flapping their wings to go against gravity. They did the best they could and they managed to give them a lighter landing but both Chelsea and Leeloo hit the ground exhausted and unable to battle.

Seert was glad that she managed to save her two comrades but she was so focused on helping them, that the Mad King appeared behind her and used his dark magic to knock her out.

"SEERT!" Charlotte yelled as she saw her friend fall before her eyes. She was about to take on the Mad King by herself but she didn't have a weapon.

"Here, take these!" Guranjan tossed Charlotte a couple of daggers she had stashed away in her bag. Charlotte thanked the shopkeeper for being so resourceful and immediately ran to take on her arch-nemesis.

The Mad King was now standing above Seert contemplating whether to finish her off but in his indecisiveness, a giant fist blindsided the Mad King.

He looked up to see Jett's shadow beast staring down at him. Not giving him a chance to recover, Jett commanded the shadow to clap his hands to squish the Mad King.

Unfortunately, the shadow couldn't clasp his hands together because Desolator had transformed again and this time, into a bo staff. The Mad King used it to prevent himself from getting squished. This gave him the time he needed to dash in front of Jett and knock him down with his fist. And as Jett fell, so too did his shadow beast.

Seeing Jett could cause him further problems, The Mad King figured he had better deal with the issue now but Charlotte had finally arrived and kicked him aside. She thanked Jett for saving Seert and once again she was facing down her mortal enemy.

Desolator changed into a pair of scrap claws, one for each of the Mad King's hands. Armed with his new weapons, he engaged in battle against Charlotte. The daggers and claws clashed against each other many times without either one wanting to give the upper hand. In comparison to every other fight, Charlotte seemed the closest to the Mad King's skill level.

Seeing an opening, Charlotte threw one of her daggers at the Mad King, who deflected it away with his claws. However, that left the King vulnerable as Charlotte appeared behind him and thought she had a clear hit. But the Mad King spun his entire body around, surprising Charlotte as her face was about to make contact with one of his claws.

Luckily, Charlotte's face barely avoided getting swiped by the claws but the Mad King elbowed her to the ground. He used his dark magic to keep Charlotte pinned. Charlotte was about to meet her demise against the claws of the Mad King but he got distracted as Nathan came yelling at him and blocked the claws with his giant sword.

Nathan was low on energy but he did his best to protect Charlotte. He was about to be overpowered but the Mad King suddenly got punched many times in swift succession. It was Zaid who still had some of his speed despite losing the mark.

That was enough of a distraction for Nathan to push the Mad King back. Once some separation was created, Annabelle zoomed in and slashed his legs. His mobility was now limited and with his attention so focused on Annabelle,

Naaz charged in and grabbed him. She swung him around a couple of times before throwing him into the air.

With the Mad King up in the air, Rhyen lined up his shot and he prepared a special arrow just for this occasion. He released the arrow at his target and upon impact, the arrow exploded and descending from the sky was the Mad King who slammed against the ground with tremendous force.

They all waited vigilantly for the result of their efforts but before the smoke could clear, a massive dark shockwave was shot out and it landed hits on Zaid, Rhyen and Nathan. Naaz, Annabelle, and Charlotte, managed to avoid the initial attack but they could not escape the second attempt. The Mad King cast his dark chain magic and had the three shackled up.

Desolator now switched into a sword that was pulsating with dark energy. The Mad King was done playing around and he needed to make an example by dealing with three of the resistance's strongest fighters. With one swing of Desolator, a destructive energy wave was about to vanquish Naaz, Annabelle and Charlotte.

The energy made a hit but it wasn't on the intended targets. Standing in front of the three women were a couple of unlikely people who took the hit. Alex the mad scientist shielded Annabelle from the fatal strike while Gia attempted to use her remaining magic to protect Charlotte and Naaz.

King's Fall

Kavan was doing everything in his power to wake Bella up. He called Bella's name and even pinched her shoulders but nothing was working. He thought he was out of ideas but then he looked to the battlefield where he saw everyone fighting for their lives.

Seeing his comrades refusing to quit, Kavan was revitalized and he began looking around for other ideas. Eventually, he spotted something that could amplify his voice. He held it with both hands and began to speak through it.

"BELLA! BELLA! WAKE UP! WE NEED YOU!" Those words rang through her ears and finally, Bella's eyes were now open.

Alex's body was extremely weak as he was collapsing on the ground. Annabelle caught him before that could happen to prevent further injuries. She tried to wake him up but he would not respond.

Then there was Gia, who was on one knee. She managed to stop the attack from reaching Naaz and Charlotte, but now her own life was in danger.

"Gia! Why did you do that?" Charlotte asked in disbelief.

"Because I'm the greatest. So I have to protect everyone who…" Before she could finish, she began to faint but Charlotte caught her.

"Hey! Don't you dare think about leaving! I'm not living through my entire life knowing I owe you something!" Naaz yelled.

Gia was now unconscious but she kept a smile on her face. Charlotte put her on the ground to rest and did Annabelle for Alex. Charlotte, Naaz and Annabelle then turned to face the Mad King, but their strength was nearly depleted and the Mad King knew it.

He was about to raise Desolator and cast another deadly shockwave but a spear was thrown just before where he stood. Everyone who saw Bella was thrilled about her return. Even the Mad King was somewhat amused to see her face again.

He was anticipating a grand rematch against his previous rival, the legendary warrior. Desolator was held up high and then he swung the blade down, blasting another dark energy wave at Bella. It made contact with her and caused a massive explosion on impact.

Everyone was disheartened to see what had happened. "Tch, what an absolute letdown. I was expecting more of a challenge. Guess, I will..." The smoke cleared and somehow, Bella escaped the attack unscathed.

Once again, the Mad King was intrigued he began to charge towards Bella. Seeing her comrade unarmed, Guranjan scoured her bag and passed her a spear, which Bella caught with her right hand. Right when the Mad King swung Desolator at her, Bella blocked the attack with her spear.

"Come on! Bring him out!" The Mad King demanded.

"Ha, I won't need him to defeat the likes of you."

Somehow, Bella was holding her own against him and not only that, seeing her stand up against the Mad King gave her comrades strength. The first person to get back some of her energy was Olivia. She used what she had left to cast a healing spell that affected most of her allies, giving them all the ability to fight again.

The Mad King was so focused on trying to defeat Bella that he didn't notice what was going on. It took a moment for the two to separate from their stalemate before he suddenly saw that all the fighters he had defeated were standing once again.

"This is impossible! But no matter, I defeated you all once before. I WILL DO IT AGAIN!"

He was about to swing with all his might to create the most catastrophe attack he could muster but Charlotte quickly prevented him from doing so by holding up Desolator with her two daggers. The Mad King attempted to overpower her but this time Naaz jumped in and threw a punch that pushed him back.

He was winded for a moment but after he caught his breath, he was ready to slam his devastating strike but surprising him was Jett's shadow beast that had him completely restrained. Desolator was about to transform to help the Mad King out of his predicament but Rylin and Rianna popped out and both attacked Desolator with their weapons. Their efforts disrupted Desolator from changing forms temporarily so the Mad King resorted to unleashing a loud warcry that sent Rylin, Rianna, and Jett's shadow flying away.

Freed from the minor annoyance, he attempted to swing Desolator again but Rhyen kept up the pressure by firing a steady stream of arrows towards him. This forced him to block with Desolator and stay on the defensive. While he was distracted, Sebastian returned with Coco who ran over the Mad King and allowed Sebastian to steal Desolator.

"Hey everyone, look! I got it! I got... oof!" Getting overly excited, the Mad King used his dark magic to tangle Coco's legs, forcing the companion to trip and Sebastian to faceplant on the ground. Not only that, Desolator was now up for grabs and the Mad King was within reach to reclaim it.

But Zaid's super speed allowed him to reach the blade before the King. He grabbed a hold of the sword and tried to run away as far as he could. Again the Mad King used his magic and the ground beneath Zaid's feet suddenly turned all muddy and he began to sink. Not wanting the King to get his hands on the all-powerful weapon, Zaid threw Desolator away and Zoë who was on her stallion, grabbed the sword and kept it away.

The Mad King was annoyed with their game of keep away and he channelled all his energy and released an outburst of energy that struck Zaid and also knocked Zoë off her steed. Once again, the Mad King was inches away from picking up Desolator but standing near it was Ava who was armed with nothing except her smile.

He told Ava to step aside but she continued to stand still. Unhappy with her disobedience, the Mad King was about to attack her but as he took a step forward, he tripped over a hole and Ava was unharmed. Everyone was relieved when they saw how lucky Ava was but the Mad King quickly got back on his feet and was ready to attack her again.

He was about to swing his sword but Kavan appeared and blew the warhorn right beside the Mad King, interrupting his rhythm. Because of Kavan's efforts, he allowed Ava to get out of harm's way.

When the Mad King regained his hearing, the first thing he saw was Chelsea holding her sword out to challenge him. He willingly accepted but what he didn't notice was that Chelsea's sword was burning up. It had been infused with Leeloo's fire.

When the swords clashed the Mad King noticed the difference. He felt Desolator being pushed back and he could feel the heat of the fire emulating from the sword. Chelsea seemed to have the advantage but the Mad King empowered himself with another spell, giving him more energy to fight back.

Even with Leeloo's flame and Chelsea's fighting skills, she was getting pushed back but as the Mad King was going for the fatal strike, Annabelle and Charlotte both appeared and blocked the Desolator from reaching Chelsea.

Annabelle, Charlotte and Chelsea combined their efforts, alternating their attack patterns to throw the Mad King off rhythm. It was working as the Mad King couldn't predict their movement and so Desolator never touched them once. Eventually, fatigue began to set in and the Mad King's speed was decreasing.

For the first time in a long while, the Mad King was worried about his survival. With this in mind, he knew he had to end the battle quickly. He launched an energy wave from his sword hoping to strike out all three fighters at once but they immediately disappeared from his sight.

As his attack missed he saw two mages and a little dragon flying over them. Twin mages Olivia and Vance performed their motto once more before Vance cast a lightning spell and Olivia cast a water spell. Then Leeloo unleashed her fire breath and the three attacks fused and struck the Mad King, shattering his armour.

Despite being in his weakened state, the Mad King somehow managed to get back on his feet. His grip on Desolator was much weaker but he still had the strength to fight. He looked back on the battlefield and something that he was not expecting. Bella was standing in ready position, with Nathan holding his giant sword tightly.

"You ready?" Bella asked.

"For once, I am. LET'S DO THIS!" Nathan replied with unyielding zeal.

Bella picked Nathan up with both hands, winding up her arm and then with all her might she threw Nathan at the Mad King. Nathan let out his signature warcry while using his whirlwind technique. The Mad King tried to use Desolator to transform but nothing happened, it appeared Desolator would no longer listen to him.

Seeing his weapon could not change forms, the Mad King desperately held out the blade to block the oncoming assault. But his grip was so weak, that the blade flew out of his hands as Nathan delivered the final blow.

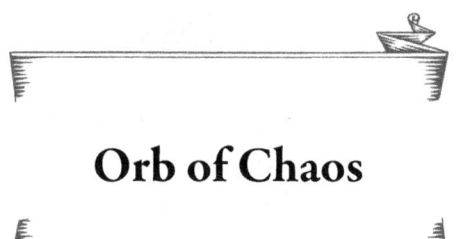

Orb of Chaos

Time felt like it stood still for the Mad King. A rush of memories appeared to him, times when he wasn't a king yet and how at a young age he hated rules and order. He found everything in the royal palace too restricting, being told rules were there to keep everyone safe, but he saw it as a prison to keep everyone locked away.

He vowed that when he became king, he would create a world with true freedom. Of course, no one else from the realm could agree with his vision. Therefore he lacked the resources to accomplish his mission until he acquired knowledge about a sacred relic known as Desolator.

Through a gruelling journey into the shadowlands, he found Desolator hidden within the depths of a forbidden temple. Before him was the answer to everything he wanted. With the sacred relic, he would be able to accomplish his vision, a realm that was free from the prison that held them back.

Unfortunately, when he made contact with Desolator, it corrupted his mind. He went mad and his vision became clouded. The relic fed on his desire to abolish the world of law and order, and so he became to be known as the Mad King and what he wanted more than anything was CHAOS.

When his mind returned to the battlefield, Nathan's giant sword struck him and delivered a fatal wound. He fell to one knee and looked around at the brave warriors who had defeated him. But the one that caught his attention most was Bella.

"You... Legendary Warrior. If you hadn't shown up, I would have..."

Upon hearing what the Mad King said, everyone immediately turned to Bella. Most of them were confused to hear him calling their friend the 'Legendary Warrior.' Bella stepped up to meet with the Mad King and she was about to speak but the voice was not hers.

"You are quite too flattering your 'Highness.'"

"What do you mean?"

"Your memory has failed you. There is no legendary warrior." Everyone, including the Mad King, was shocked.

"Impossible! There is a legendary warrior! You are the legendary warrior! That's how you were able to defeat me!"

"No. Just like how you lied about the legendary warrior's soul being shattered into four pieces, you also created another lie that you seemed to have forgotten."

"Wait, then if you never were the legendary warrior, how did you defeat me before!"

"I didn't. I was just a regular soldier whose main goal was to act as a decoy and draw your attention away."

"Then that means..."

"You didn't lose to any legendary warrior. Just like before, you lost because a small group of courageous warriors chose to stand up to your tyranny. History has a funny way of repeating itself."

At that point, the Mad King's memories began to return and he remembered everything. How he fell in battle today was similar to how he lost many years ago. In his final moments, he put his hands on his face and laughed hysterically. He truly lived up to the name of the Mad King as his body turned to ashes in the wind.

With the Mad King gone, Bella who was still under the influence of the legendary warrior's soul turned to face everyone. He told everyone that everything he told the Mad King was honest and true. He was never the legendary warrior but just a regular soldier named Rice. He said they were the true heroes and he let them know how proud he was of all of them.

Before his soul was about to disappear, Kavan told Rice to wait. He stopped for a moment as Annabelle and Guranjan carried over the unconscious mad scientist who was in terrible condition. Then shortly after, Jett's shadow's beast helped carry Gia and Admiral Sam. They were placed near one another.

Everyone began to ask Rice if he could heal everyone and bring them back. They did everything to stabilize their condition and give them potions but none of it had any effect. Even Olivia's healing magic would not work and they were out of options. Rice just smiles at them and replies, "You should check his hair." and then he vanishes.

Annabelle looked around Alex's head and found a flask hidden there. She pulled it out and saw the elixir that he was rambling about earlier. She noticed that the content had already been partially used, most likely on Zaid, Rhyen, Naaz, and herself. There was more than enough to share between Alex, Gia, and Sam.

After receiving a bit of the elixir, all three of them opened their eyes. Admiral Sam was in a relatively calm state but the same could not be said about the other two.

Alex was jumping up and down, bragging to Annabelle, "MUHAHAHA! See? I told you it would work!"

"Sigh, I think I liked it better when you were quiet."

And then there was Gia, "That's right everyone! I'm the greatest there ever was! Took a full blast from that whacko king and look, not even a scratch on me."

"You want a scratch? I will give you more than just a scratch!" Replied Naaz.

Everyone else was laughing at their banter and it seemed peace had been restored to Diamondlot, but it wasn't over yet. While everyone was celebrating and in good spirits, Kavan noticed something odd happening with Desolator.

The sword was floating in the air as if it had a mind of its own. It even had its target set in sight and it went directly towards it. When Kavan saw what was happening, he yelled and interrupted their celebration. They now all saw the possessed sword flying right at its intended target, the queen.

Nobody was close enough to help Victoria but Zaid ran as fast as he could and now he stood in front of Victoria but he was completely unarmed. Thankfully, Gurajan quickly scoured through her inventory and found a shield which she threw and Zaid caught just in time to deflect the blade of the corrupted sword.

After Zaid's successful efforts in saving the queen, everyone let out a huge sigh of relief but the battle was not yet over. Desolator, having failed to take out Victoria, suddenly transformed one last time. Everyone was bracing themselves for what terrifying weapon was about to emerge but it was something none of the warriors were expecting.

When the metamorphosis was complete, a spherical object was floating in mid-air. It was glowing and infused with a massive amount of dark energy that anyone could sense from miles away. Some of the warriors ready their weapons but Admiral Sam told everyone to stand down. She appeared to know what the mysterious object was and she began to share with everyone.

She heard tales and read many history books that mentioned an artifact known as the Orb of Chaos. Despite its size, it had the energy to destroy entire realms and even a large chunk of a planet. Not only was its power vast but there were many warnings in all she had read that if handled improperly, the Orb could denote upon contact.

Everyone waited for Sam to continue, hoping she had a solution to their current crisis but in everything she read, no civilization that encountered the Chaos Orb managed to stop it. The atmosphere suddenly felt gloomy but one person in the group had an idea. Alex the Mad Scientist pointed up into the sky and suggested that it could be possible to throw the Orb into the skies and get it as far away as possible before the detonation.

Immediately, Chelsea had her arms up as she stood in front of Leeloo. "No! We are not getting Leeloo to fly up there! It's way too dangerous!"

"She doesn't have to." Zoë interceded. "We can use one of the griffins in the stable."

"HEY! I put in hard work to raise those griffins and I love them all!" Sebastian grumbled but Kavan tried to reason with him. "Come on Sebastian, there has to be one that you don't like that much." Sebastian thought for a moment. "I guess Stink-Feathers sort of has a bad attitude." So the caretaker began to make his way back to the stable on his bullboar to retrieve one of his griffins.

While Sebastian was away, there was still one tough decision that had to be made but many were afraid to ask. So the queen stepped forward, "Alex, your plans require someone to get the orb up there. Which means…?" The Mad Scientist nodded in silence but everyone knew what he meant. There was a brief silence between everyone but eventually, someone broke the ice.

"I'll go." Everyone's eyes fell on Charlotte. "For years I served under the Mad King's tyranny and I have done some unforgivable deeds." However, Seert refused to allow that to happen. If there would ever be another attack on the realm of Diamondlot, Charlotte would be needed to stop the threat.

"I'll go." Victoria stepped up. "My time as Queen is limited and there was little I could do during the time of battle when you all needed me most." But Zoë and Ava immediately stopped her. They knew Fifthguard would be completely lost without the Queen's guidance.

There were a couple of others who volunteered to go but as everyone was still arguing, Bella had already taken the orb into her hands before anyone had noticed. She felt a massive sting as her body tried to resist the massive aura of energy that was surging from the orb. Everyone immediately rushed to her but she held out her arms and asked everyone to keep their distance.

"BELLA, what are you doing?!? Are you crazy?!?!" Nathan shouted and others did too but Bella asked for their silence as they listened to her speak.

"I know you would have all tried to talk me out of this, but it makes the most sense for me to do this." She replied.

"But why?" Chelsea asked as Leeloo looked at her with sad eyes.

Bella began to explain her situation to everyone. She had already once lost her life but had been given a second chance because of the presence of Rice's soul. Her story hit the hearts of everyone and they were left with few words.

"Bella, you won't be able to hold onto that orb forever, your body will give out." Admiral Sam informed her but Naaz took off her gauntlets that she received from Guranjan.

Naaz threw the gauntlet and Bella caught it with one hand and put them on. Thanks to the armour, she was able to resist the power from the orb more effectively. Also during that time, Sebastian had returned and he commanded his griffin to fly and land in front of Bella. She got on the griffin and looked at everyone briefly. "Thank you, everyone." The griffin took off and Bella disappeared into the air.

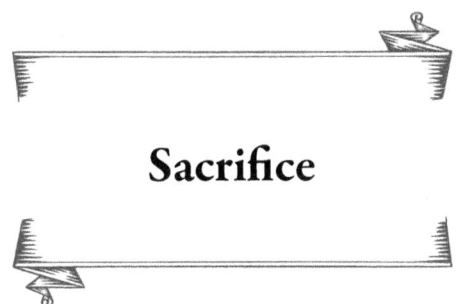

Sacrifice

The skies were filled with darkened clouds as a storm was approaching. Bella kept the orb tightly held in her hands as the Orb of Chaos grew more volatile. It was most likely what was causing the storm to brew in the sky.

As she continued to ascend, rain began to fall, making the flight more difficult. The wind blew violently, preventing her from gaining much elevation but she and the griffin pushed through. Then came the thunder which startled the griffin but Bella remained determined and her courage allowed the griffin to continue.

They were hoping to pierce through the clouds and escape the lightning but as they got higher, the air grew thinner and Bella's lungs hadn't had time to adjust. She did her best to power through but breathing was getting difficult and she was beginning to feel light-headed.

Her eyes were beginning to close but a lightning bolt that barely missed woke her up. But the griffin was startled and in its panic, caused the orb to slip out of Bella's hands. She tried to reach for the orb but her hands just missed it. She did her best to calm the griffin down so he would listen to her but it was no use. Bella watched as the orb slowly descended back onto the Earth.

All hope seemed lost but suddenly she saw the orb rising back up towards her. Carrying the orb was someone familiar to Bella.

"Someone has an extreme case of butterfingers."

"Rice!" Bella was glad to see him again with the orb in his hands. She also wondered how in the world he was floating in mid-air but there was a more pressing matter at hand. She reached out to grab the orb from him but he kept it away from her.

"What are you doing? Wait, you aren't... NO!" She attempted to fight him back for the orb but she was unsuccessful. "I should be the one to do this. I'm not even..."

"Really? Do you think that's true?" His question caused her to pause. "You might have looked away but I know you saw the look on everyone's face before you left. Despite what you think, how you brought everyone together and made them feel, that's what makes you truly alive."

Bella couldn't disagree with him but she still had words to speak. "But you are the legendary warrior, everyone needs..."

"Like I said before, I'm just a normal warrior like all of you. I've had my chance at life. Now it's time you go live yours."

Without any resistance, she replied, "Thank you."

"Go. Your friends await your return."

They went their separate ways, Rice took the orb further into the skies while Bella turned around with the griffin and began descending back to Fifthguard. However, as the griffin was slowly flying back down, a lightning bolt struck the griffin, knocking Bella off and causing her to rapidly drop down to the Earth.

Back on Fifthguard, everyone was still waiting in the area for something to happen in the sky. Ava noticed something was falling and thought it was a bird. When everyone's attention was drawn to what Ava saw, they realized it wasn't a bird, it was Bella dropping from the sky.

They all looked at each other hoping someone had a plan and it was Charlotte who was first to speak. She asked Gia if she had any energy left and she proudly stood up and used her magic to make Leeloo grow again. Chelsea and Charlotte immediately hopped onto Leeloo's back and she took off with the two warriors into the skies.

While they were gone, Zoë asked Guranjan if there was anything in her bag that could act as a soft landing. The shopkeeper searched her bag and found nothing but Ava suggested, "Why don't we just use that giant flag up there?" Zoë gave her a big hug and said she was a genius. Zaid then told everyone that he would quickly return as he rushed off towards the flag with his speed.

While Zaid was away, Alex pulled out a piece of paper along with a pencil from his hair and began writing out some crazy calculations. "Alex, we don't have time for your hair-brain science ideas." To that he responded. "Annabelle, how dare you! I'm trying to figure out where exactly they are going to land."

"Oh, I'm sorry."

"Shhhh, I require silence."

Up in the sky, Leeloo had flown against the rain and wind. She got to the point where they could see Bella falling and she attempted to catch her but another lightning came in between them and prevented her from reaching Bella.

There was too much lightning to get close to Bella so Chelsea pulled out her rope and attempted to throw it at Bella but the rain made it too difficult to get the proper aim. With time running out, Charlotte took the rope and tied it to herself instead. Chelsea, realizing what Charlotte was trying to do, attempted to stop her but it was too late as Charlotte jumped off Leeloo's back.

As Charlotte dove towards Bella, Chelsea quickly grabbed the other end of the rope before there was none left. Charlotte managed to reach Bella and once she had one arm wrapped around her, Chelsea told Leeloo to begin flapping her wings to slow their descent.

Everything was going according to plan until another bolt struck the rope and ripped it apart. Now both Bella and Charlotte were falling together and headed straight for the ground but there was something beneath them.

Seert, Zoë, Nathan, Victoria, Naaz, Annabelle, Jett, Rianna, Rylin, Guranjan, Kavan, Sebastian, Zaid and Ava gathered around to hold the flag and stretch it out. Beneath the flag were Gia, Olivia, and Vance who were standing and waiting for instructions. Alex kept looking at his calculation and then back to where Charlotte and Bella were. When they were at the height he calculated, he gave the signal to everyone.

Everyone held the flag tightly while Gia, Olivia, and Vance all cast their wind magic to create a giant updraft beneath the flag. When Charlotte and Bella hit the flag, their bodies gently landed on it, thanks to everyone's efforts.

Once the flag was slowly deflated, Bella began to wake up. "CHARLOTTE!" She yelled in excitement as she gave her a big hug. Charlotte was initially unamused, but she realized she was very happy to see her return.

Soon after, Leeloo landed safely on the ground and allowed Chelsea to hop off. Gia's magic wore off and Leeloo returned to her original size and rushed over to lick Bella on the face. Shortly after, everyone gathered and gave a massive group hug.

As the moment slowly faded away, some of them wondered how Bella was able to return to them without the orb. Bella went silent as she had a difficult time finding the words but as she was struggling, a bright explosion of colours appeared in the sky. The orb of chaos had detonated out in space and there was a faint spirit that materialized before them.

"Thank you Diamond Squad. Because of your efforts, Fifthguard and all of Diamondlot are at peace." They all recognized Rice's voice and acknowledged his efforts to save them as the final remnant of his soul faded away.

Diamond Squad

With the threat of the Mad King and Desolator gone, the world of Diamondlot was finally at rest. The Diamond Squad members were spread throughout the realm as they helped keep order in different regions.

Returning to the town of Anjen were Alex and Annabelle along with Guranjan. The shopkeeper expanded into Anjen and opened up her new business there. Annabelle would continue her mercenary work during the night and help up at Guranjan's new shop during the day. And then there was Alex who had a laboratory underneath. He hid here on most days despite the town now celebrating him as a hero ever since he discovered a cure after the events of the Swarm Lord.

Rhyen returned to his cabin alone as Olivia and Vance elected to explore the city of Fifthguard. They were welcomed as honorary members of Diamond Squad but their sibling rivalry never changed as Vance continued to make silly jokes and Olivia smacked him in the head.

Zaid wanted to test the limit of his speed so he decided to run around the entire realm of Diamondlot. He just kept running and running barely ever stopping.

The Gladiator Games continued to happen with the only two returning fighters being Jett and Rylin. Kavan continued to be the announcer of the games but there was also a new addition to the games, Gia. She found a place where she could show off her amazing spell-casting skills to a large audience. Though she had to compete against Rylin's constant reminders that he was the champion and Jett's temper that allowed him to summon his rampaging shadow beast.

Sebastian decided to set all the animals he was taking care of, free. He released them all into the wild except for Coco. Alongside his bullboar, they rode off to begin a new adventure to save other animals in need.

Victoria remained the Queen for a few more years, helping restore order and balance throughout the realm. Through her hard work and loudness, Rianna rose in the ranks and became one of the queen's royal guards. Zoë also stayed as the advisor to the queen but decided she could use some extra assistants. She got Ava to become the 'negotiator' and Naaz became the enforcer of Fifthguard. And in a pleasant turn of events, Bo and Doof turned from their terrible ways and helped rebuild the city of Fifthguard.

Seert decided to monetize her skills and so she decided to start up her own fortune-telling business in Fifthguard. It wasn't expected at first but her business drew quite the crowd and she did quite well for herself.

After taking a lap around the skies of Fifthguard, Leeloo, who was now a full-grown dragon, made a perfect landing on the ground. Hopping off her was Chelsea who was waiting for her friends to show up. From the distance, she could see Charlotte running away at top speed while Bella happily chased after her while yelling "CHARLOTTE!" Following closely behind her was Nathan who was shouting random noises as he always did.

Chelsea and Leeloo looked at each other for a moment before Chelsea spoke. "Sigh, here we go again. Alright, let's go after them and find out what trouble they will attract this time..." She hopped onto Leeloo and she took off and followed after them into a new adventure.

This is what became of the members of Diamond Squad. They disperse throughout the land helping to restore it into a better world. But if the world ever needed them again, they would come together and save the world just like they did many years ago.

Art Done by the Students!

By: Alex

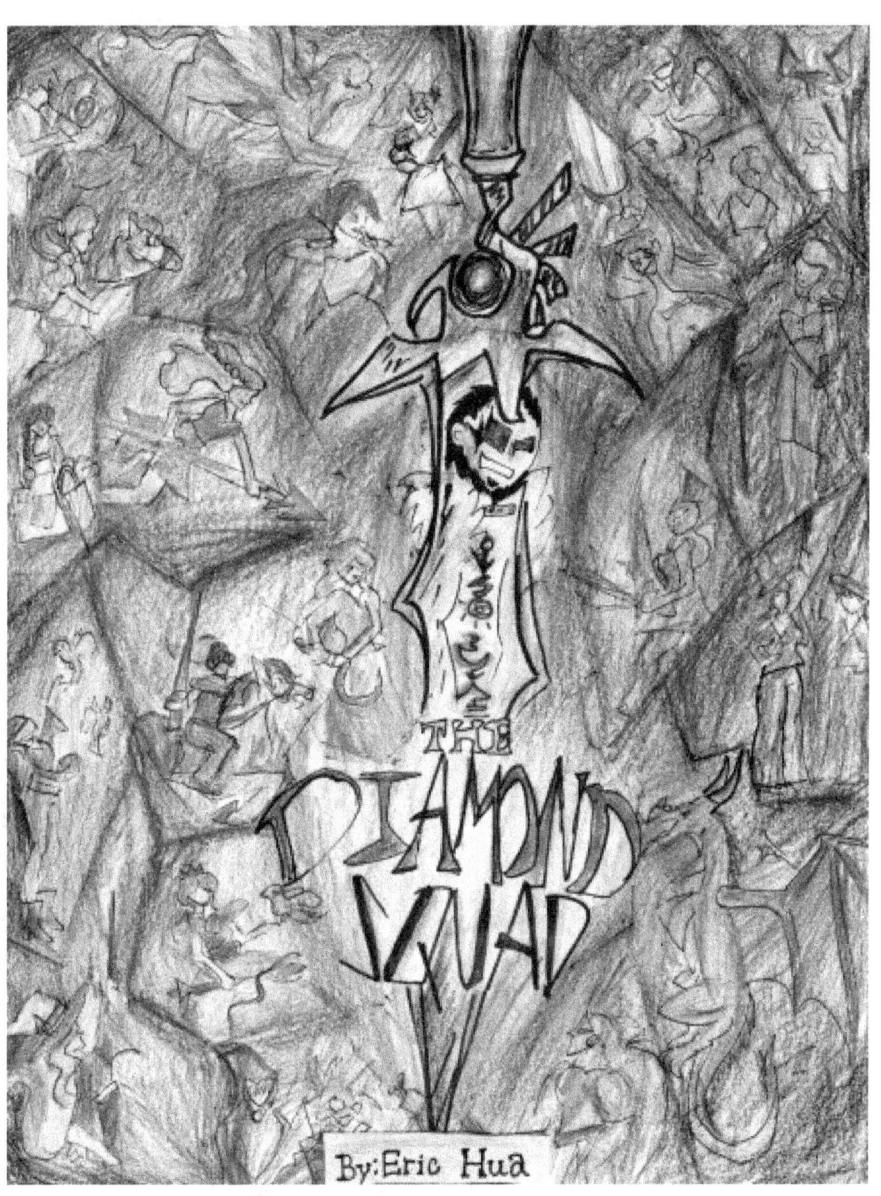

By: Chelsea

By: Victoria

By: Annabelle

By: Leeloo

By: Leeloo

About the Author

Eric is a teacher out in Surrey, British Columbia. He enjoys writing books that include his students as characters in the stories. He also enjoys playing basketball and exercising.

Printed in the USA
CPSIA information can be obtained
at www.ICGtesting.com
LVHW050421060224
770911LV00007B/189

9 798223 763499